Dhan Gopal Mukherji (1890–1936) grew up in Bengal, before he moved to Japan and then the United States. In the US he started his writing career and went on to win much acclaim for his books. He wrote a number of books for children, including the prestigious Newbery Medal-winning *Gay-Neck, the Story of a Pigeon* (1927). His children's books include *Kari the Elephant*, *Hari the Jungle Lad*, *Ghond the Hunter*, *Hindu Fables*, *Fierce Face*, among others.

THE ADVENTURES OF SIRDAR

The Chief of the Herd

DHAN GOPAL MUKHERJI

talking CUB
An Imprint of Speaking Tiger Books

SPEAKING TIGER PUBLISHING PVT. LTD
125A, Ground Floor, Shahpur Jat,
Near Asiad Village, New Delhi 110049

This edition published in paperback by Talking Cub in
Speaking Tiger Books 2023

ISBN: 978-93-5447-502-3
eISBN: 978-93-5447-503-0

10 9 8 7 6 5 4 3 2 1

Typeset in Adobe Garamond Pro by Jojy Philip
Printed at Shree Maitrey Printech Pvt. Ltd., Noida

contents

1

how the chief was chosen

Though Sirdar was one of the young elephants, without any hesitation the herd made him their chief. This was contrary to all precedent. But it had to be done because the crisis at hand was too great.

After all, to Sirdar they not only owed their escape from capture, but also from death. Out of sheer gratitude and respect for his ability they chose him their leader. In the history of the herd no one only thirty years old had been given that honour before. In fact none of the aged elephants could recall electing a chief who had not seen at least fifty summers. They said, however, 'Sirdar is young in years but old in intelligence.' That unusual things happen even among elephants is an old adage. And the series of events that led up to Sirdar's election were most unusual.

One day early in the morning the herd had scented the presence of their eternal enemy—man. The more they moved away from that scent, the nearer it drew. No matter which way they turned they were faced with the presence of man. They felt caught in a ring of humanity. Every member of the herd—calf, cow, and bull—switched their trunk east, west and north in order to locate in one direction an inch of air that was not charged with the odour of men. Alas! there was none! What were they to do now? Whither must they run for safety and cover? Their ancient chief, ninety-five years old, decided to go north. A fatal decision, no doubt; but they had to obey as soldiers obey a general. Everyone knew that they were exposing themselves too much, for only a mile to the north of them was open country. How they could hide in such a place from the pursuit of man passed their understanding. But since the way to handle a command of the chief was to obey it, they proceeded to the only direction whence, he said, came no scent of humanity. Thither must they repair first and take counsel afterwards.

Had that aged fellow put up his trunk five feet above his head, he would have learnt that in the north, too, was man and worse—a gigantic trap. Since the hunters wanted them to go northwards into the Kheddah trap, that one direction was kept free of human scent. For all the men were hiding on trees whence their odour was blown up by the wind far beyond the knowledge of the hathis. As they went north, the herd drew close to the Kheddah. All the expert elephant trappers of India had come this year armed with high-power rifles, with the intent to kill all the bulls. They were hiding on tree-tops in order to be able to aim carefully at the most vulnerable parts of the elephant's head. The entire herd knew nothing of that. The hunters' purpose was twofold; they meant to capture most of the herd and to kill those bulls who might flee the Kheddah. Since the males of this particular herd had the best tusks in India, the hunters felt all the more eager to shoot.

They surmised from their perch that the ivory they might get would be vast, for they noticed that more than one bull had tusks over five feet long, while the Chief's two *dantas,* teeth, appeared to be about seven, the longest tusks available at the time. Since this was the last year of elephant shooting in Indian history, the hunters and trappers had come prepared with the most merciless weapons. Each man felt that since the law prohibiting elephant killing was coming into force in another week's time, he must shoot as many as possible in case the herd stampeded. Business firms that dealt in Indian ivory in Paris, New York and London, had paid and armed those huntsmen to perfection. They were going to kill the most magnificent pachyderm, not that they enjoyed slaughter, but because they were hungry folks who must earn their daily bread.

After the herd had marched closer to the open country, they were called to attention by the shrill trumpeting of Sirdar who was bringing up the rear. He gave a sharp short call. The Chief snorted at the herd which meant: 'That young fool at the rear needs punishing. Follow me. March.'

Ere they had put forward another foot, the flock heard distinctly: 'Kunk—Know—Kon—man ahead, man above, about turn, retreat.'

That undisciplined cry of Sirdar enraged the Chief so that he bellowed furiously: 'Follow me—Tonk—Too.' Just then something happened that froze his muscles. In order to trumpet well, the Chief had thrown up his trunk so high that it had not only obtained the odour of man overhead, but it had literally grazed the latter's leg, knocking him down. What a shock! He went round and round quickly trampling on the wretched human. Simultaneously he trumpeted to say: 'Flee—man, man—flee. Khron—hun—Gromm.' In an instant a man from another tree shot him through the ear. The bullet proved fatal. Like a mammoth stricken, the master of the herd fell. But instead of dying like a dumb beast he used his ebbing strength for those who followed him. With his last breath he trumpeted to them: 'Ghoom—ghoon,' meaning 'Follow Sirdar.' Thus died the noble Chief. He died not a brute, but a master.

In the meantime Sirdar, who had seen a man on a nearby tree and had shouted his warning just in time, was doing all he could to lead the herd to safety in the depth of the jungle. They were all running southwards after him. Shots rang out from boughs behind and over them. Trees crashed to the ground before them as they thrust their hard heads forward. Their feet crushed all opposition under them till the thunder of their flight stilled all other sounds.

Sirdar was cool and unafraid. That is why he could extricate nearly the entire herd from the Kheddah, trap. He went on and on. With every step the stench of human presence became more and more formidable yet he pushed south, roaring, trumpeting and squealing. 'On, on, on, into the thick of that humanity. Kill the murderers, kill,' he said to himself and to his friends.

The effect of his bellowing was magical. They rushed through an army of beaters who like squirrels ran up all kinds of trees.

'So that is man,' Sirdar said to himself. 'They run faster on their two feet than we on four. How easily men take fright.'

In thirty more minutes they vanished in the depth of the jungle where man had never penetrated. As soon as they had recovered their presence of mind automatically they went to a lake not far off and washed themselves. After washing away all taint of hate and fear they came ashore.

Since a herd must not remain leaderless, they all assembled under the tall trees, and in a few minutes' time chose one. It was Sirdar—that young male who had saved and led them through dire danger. Had not the old Chief said 'Follow Sirdar'? That was enough to settle his election. 'Because we owe our lives and freedom to him, the least that we can do is to make him our Chief. Kunk, Kunk, Kunk,' they roared. Thus acclaiming him, they took their oath of allegiance to their new leader who was more humbled than pleased by such a turn of events.

2

sirdar meditates

After the election Sirdar went off all by himself to meditate upon his future. And since the future is related to the past his mind eventually went back a few years.

The reason for his doing so lay in the fact that had his past been different, he could not have reached his present position. Of all the elephants of that flock, he was the one that had had the largest contact with man. For when he was nineteen months old his father was killed for ivory and his mother captured to do work in the teak woods for a company of lumbermen. He went with his parent to live as a slave amongst men. Even now as he milled about the lake shore in the deepest jungle he thought of his three years of captivity. He recalled how he and his mother were lassoed with leather thongs, how they were starved for more than a fortnight, and last of all how, dropping with hunger and fatigue, they submitted to the tyranny of men for the sake of food. An elephant exhausted with extreme hunger submits to anyone who gives him his first meal. In this respect they do not differ from many men.

The man who fed them became their Mahout, master. Even now Sirdar remembered how he winced when the Mahout touched his trunk the first time. It was a terrible humiliation. Think of a biped, no better than a monkey, patting an elephant's trunk! But he and his mother were so famished that they had to put up with everything inflicted on them by their captor, the Mahout, provided that it brought them food, more food, whether it be twigs of trees, rice of hay. The pain of hunger stung their vitals like a thousand vipers.

'But, thank the gods of the elephants that captivity taught me what men are and how they act,' he said to himself. 'Had I not known man intimately, I could not have detected his presence on the tree this morning. I succeeded in eluding man's cunning because of my knowledge of his habits. Man hides in trees like monkeys.'

Now he recalled the odours of man and his village. If man was happy and unafraid he smelt like trees—nice and friendly; if he was angry and afraid—anger and fear go together—man gave forth the odour of dead things. And it was invariably during the times that the Mahout was afraid that he brought on the elephants all kinds of suffering. He hurt them with the *ankus,* and beat them behind their ears with his heel. Think of somebody hitting under your ear, making you dizzy with strange pains. That is how man punishes elephants for the slightest error of the latter. What a life! At last, unable to bear it any longer, Sirdar and his mother decided to run away into the jungle. Of course they knew that they could not plan it for they had not brains enough for that. But they acted on impulse. And that worked like a well-planned scheme.

One day the Mahout had gone into the deep jungle with his two hathis. There they were made to drag logs that had been hewn by wood-fellers the previous day.

They not only dragged the logs to a far-away place which ox-carts could reach, but they had to arrange them on the carts all in an even pile. Imagine logs a ton apiece having to be piled one upon the other like match-sticks in a box. Whenever one log stuck out too far from the rest, the mother put her head against it, then Sirdar putting his head behind her, they pushed with all their might. It bruised the mother's head badly and Sirdar's neck hurt, yet they were forced to push till the log ceased to stick out.

And whenever they failed to do their task well, the Mahout hit them behind their ears. Sometimes he jabbed the mother's neck with the sharp ankus. Towards noon that March day already mentioned they were hurt so that they felt all the more the call of the jungle. Spring voices hummed in their ears. Birds above cooed and cried like many-tongued temptations. Thus the witchery of the wood entered their eyes, their ears, their very souls.

Flowers filled their nostrils with ravishing fragrance. Orchids large as maple leaves shook their pollen on the tip of their trunks. Lotus leaves large as their ears lay like trays of emeralds in silver pools. And lotuses big as the moon poured intoxication into the already fragrant air. Spring, spring, spring, hummed the gold-black bees as they strung their flights from flower to flower. Each tree or sapling they tasted oozed with sap. Nature put her lips to their aching ears and whispered, 'Flee, flee, flee to freedom. Leave this man to his wood-piling. You are in the depths of the forest; if you run a mile away to the east he can never find you. Fly.' 'Coo, coo, coo,' cried the kokil as she deposited her eggs in a crow's nest. 'Tia—tia, tia, tia, tia-ta,' whistled the Papia thrush, in silver notes of beauty. 'Run, run, run,' whispered the breeze. Who could resist such temptation? Spring was calling both mother and son.... Spring....

Just that very moment their master did something foolish. He spat on the big elephant's trunk as she was lifting it to the tree overhead for a twig to eat. That made her act as if she had been hit by the thunderbolt. She trumpeted shrilly, then flung forward, her bruised and aching head breaking a thick peepul tree. The man on her neck dug the ankus deep into her, but instead of stopping her, it drove her on all the faster. That instant a heavy branch of a tree under which the big elephant passed swept the man off her neck. Her son following after nimbly skipped over the dead Mahout. Like a lioness set free she ran, leading Sirdar. Now, after many years Sirdar could not recall whether in his mad rush he had really skipped over the fallen man. All that he remembered now was Spring commanding him 'Run, run, run.' Even the grass under his feet said 'Run, you are free, you are free.' And it did not take him long to know that they were both truly free.

After their escape they spent three years all by themselves. During that time the mother taught the son all that she knew of man, beasts and trees. Among animals who have no schools every bit of instruction is given to the child by its mother. That makes a mother's life quite hard. In the fourth year came into their life a tusker, Sirdar's step-father, scarred and branded with marks of conquest. He was indeed a conqueror. The old fellow had come prepared to fight for his mate. For that was his way of winning his cow. His long scars like stripes of glory told Sirdar that here indeed was a tusker worthy enough to take his father's place.

The old warrior filled that position well. He taught Sirdar all the twist of trunk and the thrust of tusks that he knew. In two years' time just after his step-sister's birth Sirdar left them. Now he roamed alone, seeking for a suitable herd to join. During that time he encountered man many times. But every occasion left him wiser and more dexterous. In time he learned that man is a tree-climber. And the safest place from which man can hurt an elephant is a tree-top. Man and tree became identical for him. That is why he always switched his trunk sideways as most elephants do and raised it frequently at least a yard above his head. He never passed under more than two trees without swinging up his long nose in the quest of the odour of fear that comes from man.

It was because of that habit formed in his early years that he was able to detect the presence of human beings in the jungle this particular morning. 'This morning,' he seemed to say to himself, 'I outwitted man just in time. Thank the gods of the elephants I formed very good habits in my boyhood. Grunt—what's that? Ah! my herd is trumpeting for me. Thinking about the past I forgot my present. Ghonta!'

That trumpet call meant 'Follow me.' And like little children the whole herd came where he was. Then, taking the foremost position, he led them in a northerly direction. Thus began Sirdar's long and strenuous task of leadership.

3

elephants and other jungle folks

As the herd moved towards the gorges of the river Brahmaputra where Spring had just begun, Sirdar became alive to the relation of his tribe to other animals. First of all its relation with the buffaloes was of the greatest importance. The latter always had a very friendly attitude towards the elephants. In fact they kept in constant touch with one another. Whenever they met, the young hathis played with the young steers. The elephants chased them most playfully. Then the buffaloes replied: they drew in their horns and charged. That instant the little pachyderms pretended to run for their very lives. They ran all the way to where their own herd was loitering. So back and forth the young of the two species played for hours. Sometimes a young elephant would place his trunk over a buffalo's head and let it slide all the way over his neck and back. It had a strange effect on the latter. He would jump off from under the trunk as soon as possible, it tickled him so!

Next to the buffaloes the elephants treated the deer and the antelopes the best. Whenever a frightened antelope came near them, they stood by and gave him the protection of their presence. That invariably scared off a tiger or any other cat that happened to molest the poor beast. It was the duty of the elephant-chief to see to this sort of aid given to frightened vegetarian quarrupeds.

Soon it became clear to Sirdar that the task of a leader can never lie in idling, eating and drinking. To protect the weak against the strong was, next to saving the life of one's own tribe, the religion of a drove of hathis. The observance of such a religion had to be enforced by the leader. So a chief of a herd of elephants is not only a king but also a priest.

One day the herd came across a vicious tiger. It promised to be an unpleasant incident. What had happened was this. A tiger about a dozen years old was running after a stag. In order to escape successfully, the deer was making for the river nearby. Between him and the big cat lay hardly ten yards. His great fear was evident to the elephants by the odour that his body, foaming with sweat, left behind him. They said to one another: 'Now that fear has gripped him the tiger can catch him. He who is frightened loses his wits and is easily killed.' The big cat leaped faster and faster reducing the space between them to twenty feet, if not less. That he had reached striking distance the tiger knew, so he charged to kill. He roared, hoping to paralyse the deer to a standstill with the thunder of his voice. Just that instant he found before him the head of an elephant. It was Sirdar who by accident had come there at the head of his herd. That made the cat most impatient. So instead of waiting to let the elephant pass, he leaped...Sirdar was surprised at his audacity. Had he not been at the head of a drove he might have lurched backwards and let the tiger land on the stag, but his duty as Chief made him stand fast. He waited, breathless and unflinching. The tiger was at the point of landing against his neck in order to claw his left ear and eye. The elephant, with the agility of a squirrel, fell on his knees. The tiger passed over him, and landed on the ground. But before he could recover from the momentum of his fall, Sirdar had not only raised himself but was in the act of putting a front foot on the poor cat's hind quarters. With a squeal of terror the brute bounded out of sight, running faster than any deer.

All that fuss and waste of minutes had given the stag a chance to run into the river. There he lay hid. With the exception of the tip of his nose and about an inch of his antlers nothing showed on the surface of the stream. And since the current of the water had washed away all sweat and odour of fear, the naturally weak scent of the tiger told him nothing of his would-be victim's whereabouts. He sniffed the air again and again but it gave him no clue. Though he searched the water before him carefully, he could not discern the tips of the stag's antlers through a screen of reeds. Just at that instant he had the greatest surprise of his life. He was turning towards the forest when lo! he was faced with a wall of hathis. A range of ebony mountains was advancing upon him. What was he to do? The earth trembled as inch by inch the herd moved forward. What was he to do? Every fraction of a second wasted in thinking brought the serried ranks of elephants closer to him. Now it was his turn to sweat with terror. But, as you know, tigers and lions are not cowards. So bending his head he charged. He dashed forward like a streak of light at Sirdar. The latter was ready. His most vulnerable spot, the tip of his trunk, was coiled and buried in his mouth. His tusks had been cleared for action. One, two, three—rearing on his hind legs he received the two hundred pounds of the cat on his tusks. Keeping his eyes and ears free of the slashing claws of the enemy, quickly he came down on his feet. Quicker still he knelt and pinned the wretched tiger to the ground. 'Hunha!' roared the tiger. After that mortal wail his body began to grow limp. Soon his muscles relaxed, his skin quivered, then his head fell back. Slowly over his topaz eyes stole the darkness of death.

Seeing that all was safe, the stag swam ashore and went off in the pursuit of his own flock from whom he had been separated. As the elephants knew, the deer were coming down from the Himalayas after wintering on its snow-clad foothills. Deer-folks go up the hill in the autumn in order to await the birth of their young. And as soon as the calves are able to run well, they begin to abandon the snowy heights in search of spring grass, since the growing young must have good food in plenty.

In the meantime Sirdar had plunged into the river to take a bath. Having cleaned himself of the traces of his last encounter, he came ashore and led the other elephants further north. Every day they saw new places and had stranger experiences. But none of them was as dramatic as their encounter with that vicious tiger.

4

in the spring pastures

Some of the trees in the northern countries were dying. Everywhere the elephants noticed that the barks of those trees about two feet above the ground had been cut almost in a ring. The scar was so deep that the timber itself was gashed in places, cutting off the flow of sap. Now the question was: 'Who killed the trees in that fashion?' It was the deer. When a deer's antlers grow, his head itches so that he rubs it against certain trees. The sharpness and the hardness of the antlers cut through the bark. Sometimes in order to get the velvet off their antlers, the deer rub and rub against a tree till they destroy all the connecting tissues of the tree through which the life-giving sap runs. That kills it in several days' time. Nature has probably arranged matters thus in order to keep trees from growing too numerous. And again it is she who sets the tiger to kill deer so that the deer do not grow to be too many.

The seeds blown by the wind seek rich soil. Then as soon as they have sprouted and grown the deer search after the rich vegetation and devour it. Next comes the tiger after his meal—the deer. Last of all man kills the tiger in order to prevent a too great increase of the cat tribe. When we look at the book of Life we find that it has many chapters. Minerals, plants, animals, man, and stars, each enriching the contents of the volume. And to our human mind animals are more interesting than inanimate nature. And of all the animals, the hathis are the most interesting to observe.

It is time that we had a roll-call of our elephant herd. Sirdar must know the number of his followers and their quality. There were sixty-three all told. Of these about fifteen were youngsters not more than twenty months old. There were eleven males below twenty and sixteen females of the same age. Out of the remaining twenty-one they had six bulls who were in the prime of their life, from forty to seventy. One of them was a bachelor, while the others had wives. The bachelor's name was Kumar. Since he and Sirdar were great friends it is wise to make a special mention of him. They were of the same age and shared many adventures together. They quarrelled only once, during a later mating season. But until that fight they remained fast friends. This particular spring the remaining ten bulls were the only ones who had come north in order to find proper mates for themselves.

Since the mating of elephants never follows a smooth course, it will be interesting to see how they won their wives.

Within two weeks of pasturing Spring was so advanced that the gorges of the Brahmaputra were choking with life. Orchids large as half a dozen roses covered the moss that lay like a thick emerald armour on the giant trees. Lilacs poured their perfume down the breeze like broken honeycombs. Bees hummed on their paths from flower to flower. If an elephant got in their way they stung him, irrespective of his impregnable hide. Sometimes his tail would knock down bees from his side as a child brushes off water drops from his body with a towel. Pythons rolled in the grass with sinister softness. Parrots clamoured and flew in flocks like a wind-blown arras of emerald. Baboons chattered and leaped from tree to tree. Eagles floated far up in the turquoise air, poised as thunderbolts of silence. Far off came the lazy growl of spring-smitten tigers. At night the fighting for food and mate smote the silences into tortured yells. The bisons bellowed. Yaks barked almost like dogs. The stag struck the echo-laden glens with the hammer of his challenge, while ten of Sirdar's unmarried bulls trumpeted and fought alien tuskers in the field of battle. Then over them all the Doel (Indian nightingale) hung the air with enchantment.

It must be borne in mind that elephants are not allowed to marry without the approval of their herd. If they do so they leave it and go to join some other herd. It is always the mating of the fit with the fit that the herd is interested in. The Chief of course sees to it that no unworthy male or female marries into his clan.

So out of ten or fifteen droves of hathis that they encountered, about seven supplied the right sort of girls for Sirdar's boys. The others, because they had fallen in love with the cows that nobody liked, had to leave their own and join their wives' clans.

Not a word was spoken; no scenes took place. Those who mated with the wrong brides had to go. Since love is stronger than patriotism they simply turned up their long noses at Sirdar and his friends, and trotted off into the darkness of the jungle with their girls. Of the mating of those whose matches were approved of, the story was dramatic. First of all they were repeatedly driven away by the females' own herd. But at last unable to bear it any longer, the young male stood his ground. Curling up his trunk, he emitted a soul-shaking challenge. That instant the strongest male of his age from the other side bellowed at him with equal force, meaning: 'I take up the challenge.'

Then began a battle royal. Trunk to trunk, tusk against tusk, foot to foot they fought. They gashed one another's legs and sides. Sometimes one of them lost a tusk, yet he fought. In the meantime the lady who was the cause of all this was breaking off the twigs of the trees nearby and eating them as if she were walking in a quiet garden. At last when the fight was over, her victorious lord took her to a lake where they enjoyed the first swim of their life together. There he fed her on lotuses as they swam. After a honeymoon of some days, the two of them returned to the bridegroom's herd. Thus the bride was made a member of the family. Within a couple of years when she became a mother, the little child became the new citizen of the old clan. But what a fine child! In order to produce a fine youngster, all that selecting at the mating time had to be gone through. The more one studies the conduct of elephants the better one realizes that not only man, but his lesser brothers, all work for quality. A human group or a drove of hathis seeks to create not quantity but descendants whose mettle is above reproach.

5

the art of leadership

Since the hero of a story must be the person who carries in his mind the real secrets of his experience, he alone can tell us about them. It is natural that Sirdar should speak to us about the art of being the Chief of the herd. For a while let us take on the character of elephants and listen to the tale that our hero has to unfold in hathi-language.

'O! beloved of felicity, O! diadem of wisdom, it is easy to be elected Chief of the herd, particularly when there are no politicians among us. From time immemorial we elephants have elected the most gifted of the flock to its leadership. But I am not yet sure that the herd has not made a mistake in my own case. He who is chosen may find in himself an abyss of weaknesses. I, who am the weakest of the weak, felt more frightened at the honour done me than I can tell you. I was indeed humbled by it.

'But, as my mother taught me, "When honoured feel humble, and occupy the seat of authority—as you grow your tusks—naturally, simply. Not elated by honour, nor troubled by dishonour must be the conduct of an elephant."

'However, the first thing that made me almost sick with excitement was when I gave my first word of command. Imagine me, hardly thirty years old, trying to trumpet as sonorously as an elephant of ninety. My heart beat so that I thought it would burst through my thick hide and spill itself on the ground. But the gods of the hathis proved benignant, for they helped me to trumpet with the force and assurance of a master. I could tell by its effect on my people that I had done it well. They, seniors as well as juniors, fell into line and followed me like a river running down a field.

'There was nothing for me to do now but to lead. So all of them came after me in single file.

'There are many reasons why we invariably go in that manner. Here I shall mention only two of them. An elephant must enter that precious emerald, the jungle, as simply as does a black thread the hole in a bead. Our body being large, in fact the largest of all the animals on land, we have to have the greatest amount of cover. A beetle may hide anywhere. But an elephant can hide only in the thick forest. If we went abreast of one another our bodies would brush out of existence many branches, saplings and boughs. Were that to happen what would give us cover? Years of experience have told us that we should make a path in the jungle as a plough does in the soil. We draw a single furrow very deep between high banks of protecting foliage and grass and, thus protected, we go in and out of the jungle.

'The second reason for our going single file is more intricate. You know that a hathi cannot move his head about as a donkey does. Our necks are riveted. We cannot look over our shoulders by turning our heads. Then there is our second weakness, our ears are large and our eyes small. Even if we could twist our neck our eyes would be prevented from seeing anything by our vast ears.

'All this makes our rear vulnerable. And the only thing that can somewhat protect it is our trunk. That delicate organ made of muscles without bones and with its hard corrugated exterior of insensitive skin, we swing behind us to catch the odour of any enemy who might be attacking us from the rear. That is why our trunks are for ever in action. Our vast size and exposed rears demand it.

'To protect our rear all the members of a herd must forego the risk of marching abreast of one another. It will expose too many backs to a wider range of danger. So what we do is to go single file; from the head of the drove to its tail, we are protected by our trunks. In case one of us gets the odour of a dangerous enemy he can telegraph it quickly to the one behind him, and he to the next, and so on till during the time of a few heart-beats the entire tribe is alert and ready to meet any trouble. No such swift action is possible otherwise. Now you know why we must travel in the usual formation. No doubt we sometimes wander in a crescent formation, but that is permissible in countries where everything is safe. Thank the gods of our race there are places where man and other killers have not yet appeared.

'The elephant has no enemy but man. The tigers generally give us no trouble. When they see us coming they go away. Once in a great while when we get in the way of their food they attack us. But that is exceptional.

'Similarly the leopards, the panthers and the cheetah, no matter how hungry, never think of dining on us.

'Alone among the vegetarian animals we are troubled by no citizen of the forest. Doubtless we hear of trouble from the rhinoceros, but they are mostly old elephants' tales. I was told once by a fellow of a hundred and ten that a rhino tried to tickle him to death by putting his horn in the old tusker's belly. When I put my trunk there I could not smell or feel any scare. So I think the whole thing was an invention? Elephants in their old age talk too much nonsense.

'Buffaloes, deer, snakes and boars, do not bother us. In the water if we float with our noses up in the air, we fear neither crocodiles nor sharks. So you see a hathi has no enemy who is jungle-born. But that is small consolation when it is the city-born ape without tail, man, who is the foe of elephants. Other beasts are harmless but he who is armed with guns is the deadliest. "Man is an animal with a gun." What horror! And though he is the greatest source of danger to all birds and beasts, yet he flatters himself by saying "I am a weak, unarmed man."

'But to return to my herd. The day after I was chosen Chief, my wits had to be matched against those of man. It happened at twilight near a lotus lake.

'You remember the men who tried to catch us in their trap. Well, some with their weapons had run far ahead of us, lying under cover. After we had marched about four miles, just as the dusk had begun to fall near the lotus lake, they started to belch forth the red sting of bullets at us. Fortunately the jungle was so thick that they hit tree trunks which they took for our bodies in the dark. Probably they did not wish to hurt, but just wanted to drive us back into their trap.

'What could I do? I, an inexperienced tusker of thirty? My dependents were growing more and more restive as the red sting passed close to them. One bullet glanced off my own back. What was I to do?

'That instant my mother's lesson came to my

mind. "Unafraid you are safe, afraid you are dead." So I mustered my forces and did what my step-father once made us do when beset by men. "Run toward the lake and do as I do," I whispered to the octogenarian behind me. He whispered the same message to the tusker that followed him. In several heart-beats' time every soul knew what they were to do. We broke through the cordon of bullets as a wind goes through a net. We did it so silently that even to mention it seems full of noise. We stole through, then, beyond the humans. I could tell by swinging my trunk that man was far behind me. Then, lo! there was the open space of the lotus-covered lake where lingered enough sunlight to betray the presence of large animals.

'But I did exactly what we had done when I was young. I slid into the water with no more noise than the bursting of a bubble. Then swimming forward I submerged my whole body save the tip of my trunk. That even I concealed. Instead of sticking it out in the open space I thrust it under a lotus leaf just above the surface of the water. One by one my friends did the same thing long before the men had learnt whither we had drifted. Tracking us down was not easy now. Though they reached the lake-shore soon enough I could tell that by the scent of man—they could not find us. Even the smallest elephant was buried under water and by the help of his periscope of a trunk could tell where the animal with the gun was moving. Many long agonizing hours passed. Time lengthens when you are in difficulty and shortens when you are in joy.

'The twilight passed. The solemn moment of silence that separates day from dark throbbed on the drum-like surface of the lake then sang into the stillness of night. Tigers roared far off, owls hooted, bats fanned the air above our heads as we swam across the lake behind the ambush of dusk. That was my first real act of leadership. Was I proud of it? I was too tired to think of it after an hour's swim. When we walked up the bank of the lake, I dismissed the herd with four sounds: "Go, eat your fill."'

6

more about leadership

Sirdar continued: 'Before I go any further I must tell you about an elephant's religion. You know that no living creature exists who does not bathe. It is also true that no creature can live without adoring the gods.

'For instance, every dawn and every sun-down, for one moment of silence, every animal stands still. He is awe-struck by the meeting at the edge of dark, or parting, at the rim of day, with his friend Surya, the sun god. The eagle in the farthest heavens, the hawks in the lower sky, the rabbit hiding at the root of the grass, the tiger crouching at his lair-mouth, the monkeys on tree-top, and the bison on the lake-shore—all watch the coming and the departure of Surya, the lotus of light.

'No animal can live without adoring the sun and his bride the moon. If you do not believe me, go, wash your eyes of ignorance, and watch the birds and beasts during twilight. At that hour strife does not raise its voice, and hunger dares not release murder abroad. Held by awe, we adore our God. As the body needs its bath, the soul needs its daily adoration. He who does not adore Surya is only half alive. Elephants, like the other animals, have their religion.

'As a leader I had to see to it that I worshipped twice a day. My soul demanded it. Otherwise I could not have led my friends.

'Now let me tell you more about leadership. The problem of food and drink is a difficult one. When you go about in a herd, each one of whose members eats about thirty to fifty pounds of twigs and grasses a day, the Chief has to think out the best routes to be taken. By tasting the lushness of a branch of a tree, you can tell whether the fodder ahead will be good and plentiful. If tree after tree tastes dry be sure that that section of the jungle has no food to offer. You must change your path and go a different way.

'Every few hours thirst seizes a herd. When migrating the Chief has to think out the whereabouts of water-holes. Generally the old Chiefs know exactly where the holes are. But a young fellow like myself who had not had much experience was obliged to ask others' help. They sometimes led the crowd for me to lakes and rivers that I had not observed during my previous travels. Water for drinking and bathing is the most important factor next to food. A leader who never pays attention to such matters will not be able to hold his place longer than two sunsets. My advice to all Chiefs, young or old, is that whenever in doubt they should take counsel from their followers, since the lives of the latter may be endangered by a false step.

'I have said that the taste of the twigs and branches of a forest tell us whether there be food enough ahead of us. Our sense of smell is also important. We can get the fragrance of water a few hundred yards away. But since our trunk is our greatest asset I shall speak of it a little later.

'Let me speak of the virtues of our ears. I think our ears are more valuable to us than our eyes. The latter are small and fixed in a certain place. If we have to look sideways we are forced to turn our body round before our eyes can focus. Because of the limitation to our sight, the gods of the elephants gave us ears that we can move. We can move our ears as a deer moves his head. Our ears are most powerful of all. Because their size happens to be very large, larger than a huge lotus-leaf, we could catch many more sounds than the other animals. We trap the most delicate noises in the net of our hearing. Even the flight of a single gnat we can hear. Inaudible though the sound be to a deer or to a panther, our ears can catch it as a spider-web traps a fly.

'That is not all. The way we always tell the difference between a sound and its echo is most dramatic. The left ear may be busy hearing the sound of the snapping of a vine on the river bank while the right one is held at an angle that can distinctly hear its echo on the waters. Had we not that gift of distinguishing sound and echo we would suffer more difficulties than we usually do.

'For instance, once I had gone all alone to a drinking place. It was a vast pond. The air there was still that noon hour. Nothing stirred to break the stillness. I put my trunk into the water as softly as a snake crawls into a hole. Just then I heard a few leaves stir overhead. Now that my nose was full of water I could not lift it up to get the odour of the creature on the branch above me. So I swiftly turned one of my ears toward the sounding board below. The echo of that slight noise in the water told me who was moving up yonder. It was a python lazily stretching himself. The sickening shiver of leaves was unmistakable. I was certain of it by the trembling echo that creased the stillness of the water.

'I took my drink in leisurely fashion, then went off in search of my companions. To tell you the truth I detested the experience. Serpents of all sizes and every shape annoy me.

'Our ears are almost as far reaching as our noses. Now let me sing the glory of the latter. That member of our body is priceless. It is three-fold in its meaning. It is our nose, our drinking tube and our hand. In fact the word Hathi comes from Hath, hand. He who carries his hand in the front of his face is known as a hathi, hand-guided animal.

'If an organ is three instruments rolled in one, it becomes very valuable. But more than this it is also our great weapon. With one stroke of our trunk we can knock down a tree. More than once I have made tracks in the thick forest by knocking down trees with my trunk. Once I broke the back of a tiger with it. This is how it happened. It was very hot in the plains one day in the latter part of summer. There was not a tree in sight anywhere. So, as is the practice of all elephants, I pulled up tufts of grass with all the mud clinging to their roots, and spread them on my back. This kept my hide cool. I felt so comfortable that I did not mind marching towards the jungle across the plain. I was walking slowly and most noiselessly. Had I only known I would have made noises that would have warned people of my coming. But as fate would have it I almost stepped on a tiger who was asleep in the grass. The shock of my coming was so great that it unhinged his mind. Instead of going away as normally elephants and tigers do from one another, he leaped up and tried to bury his teeth into that soft and delicate thing, my lower lip. What was I to do? There was not even the possibility of dodging his spring, let alone running away. I had to decide and act quickly. Since he was coming at my throat and lower lip and because a bite there might be fatal, to avoid it I risked something else. I brought down my priceless trunk and put it in front of him. It grazed his ear, and felled him to the ground.

But quicker than the stinging of a cobra he crouched and leaped again...just as he was off the ground I lashed him. "Hun, haoom—hoom," he roared. Then behold, he lay dying of a broken spine. Alas! I am ashamed to say that I had lost my head during the encounter so completely that I set about to kick him. Imagine the horror that seized me when I realized that I had reduced him to nothing. A sense of nausea dug into me like a tenfold ankus, and I ran away from the place in quest of a stream where I could wash myself. We elephants do not like to kill. If we do it, we wash away the odour of it very soon.

'Let us return to the art of leadership. It consists in holding every sense of one's body alert and thinking all the time of the needs of the herd. And the most important need of a herd is not food, nor drink. It is something entirely remote. What is that thing? Self-possession, without which there is no self-preservation.

'Let me illustrate what I have in my mind. The fourth day of my leadership told me that no drove of hathis is stronger than its weakest member. We had some young ones who could walk no more than from sunrise to sunset. Besides, they could not ford rivers more than seven feet deep. Suddenly after an all-day march without eating, instead of a good feeding place where we could spend the night, we came upon a deep gorge where the Brahmaputra ran like lions of anger. Behind us lay a very bad country, and before us a stretch of water that none could cross. The herd was hungry and tired. And everybody's temper was whetted like a tiger's claws. The young fellows whimpered and complained enough to deafen you. Food, food, food. Would they go back? No. Would they walk a little more downstream? No. They were too tired to do anything. Their little limbs ached and their bellies were a hollow of pain. What were they to do? There was nothing for it but to drink a little water and rest. That I ordered. And they obeyed. A herd may be full of amazingly powerful hathis; yet it will act like a flock of goats if its sense of self-possession does not remain firm.

'It was during our drink that we discovered under the bank a great quantity of ferns and grass. We, the old ones, plucked them by the trunkful and gave them to the young, who were only too glad to have something to chew. Then, to every three trunkfuls given to the children we gave one to their young mothers. That went on for half an hour.

'Seeing that all the young and almost all the females had satisfied at least part of their hunger, we formed the mothers into a circle which, like a ring, protected their sons and daughters who went to sleep at once. Having seen to the safety of the young, we males went into the night in quest of food and to find a path into the nearest food-pasture. Though we found very little to eat, yet we reconnoitred with such zest that we at last came upon a fine *sal* forest, full of the abundance of late Spring. By now it was midnight. Without waiting to make a meal of leaves and succulent boughs, half of us decided to go back in order to fetch the rest of the herd, while the other half I left behind under Kumar in possession of the forest. Though we were hungry and weary in the extreme, we pushed on faster and faster. In about three hours' time we reached the cows and the calves, who had been sleeping. Our coming roused them. Ere they could feel anew the pinch of hunger with the rising of the sun, I made them march as quickly as possible to the sal woods. Though famine rumbled in the stomach of all the males, though fatigue stung every muscle in their bodies like vipers, still they marched. We were determined to reach the jungle of our midnight discovery before the infants could start puling for food. And thank the gods of the hathis, we arrived there just in time. Now leaving the cows to feed their calves, all of those bulls who had toiled with me all night, fell upon the trees like locusts on a grainfield. We ate like monsters. In half an hour the trees were shorn of most of their twigs.'

7

the herd in difficulty

After the mating season was over the herd moved in many directions. They ate the June foliage of Brahmaputra plateaus and the July grass of the Tista. August found them moving slowly towards the Gangetic valley of the south.

Had they moved very fast they would have had no trouble at all. But because they travelled in the most leisurely fashion, September caught them near the Kheddah of the Rajah of Cooch, almost at the threshold of the Himalayas. The orders of the State were that since the Rajah's stud was deteriorating his Mahouts were to catch about twenty young elephants for the purpose of replenishing the royal stock; hunters had been sent out far and wide to select a drove that afforded the finest specimens. They had been told that after they had sighted the herd, they were to close in upon it and drive it into the traps. After erecting the usual wall of timber into which the herd was to be driven, the trappers had also made lassos out of thick thongs and spread them on the ground nearby. Delicious twigs had been so cleverly used to cover these traps that no elephant could tell that they were there, so successfully were they hidden out of sight and odour! It amounted to wizardry. You must not forget, however, that an elephant's keen sense of smell could generally detect under such twigs the scent of hide.

After discovering Sirdar's herd, the hunters concluded that it was about the finest single flock that they could hope to find. Certain signs showed this. The most striking thing was the beauty of each hathi's skin. It shone like polished ebony amid the jade-green foliage; now and then a shaft of sunlight fell on the backs of the herd making their hides glint like gun-metal. The very sight of it took the hunters' breath away. They whispered to one another: 'Tajjab—wonder. They move like wonder on four feet. Keyabat.' In English the last word means 'What word can describe this?' What word, indeed!

In the meantime Sirdar was getting more and more convinced that the place was haunted and tainted by man. He confided his suspicion to Kumar, who has been mentioned before, and to the very old elephants. They agreed that there was something wrong, but since none knew exactly what it was, it seemed best not to spread suspicious rumours among the rest of the tribe. So they trudged on.

In the meantime everything tasted good. Even the taste of water from some of the brooks was far better than any before. Kumar hinted to Sirdar, 'You take the leadership of the herd too seriously. You are too eager to smell danger. Whoever heard of such a critical Chief as yourself! You are getting to be an old cow.' Sirdar grunted. He knew all about Kumar's character. Happy, carefree, a perennial bachelor, Kumar did not care whether the herd got into trouble or not. So when Kumar had finished his chatter, he let silence fall between them.

Suddenly it occurred to Sirdar that the only way to find out whether man was about or not was to spread out the herd on many tracks instead of travelling single file. This idea seemed so brilliant that he acted on it. An order went forth. Elephants are quick at receiving orders and obeying their Chief. Looking at their size in a zoo, one may doubt it. But if anyone has seen herds of them change their tactics in the jungle, he will testify that those vast brutes move softly and swiftly like lizards on a rock.

According to the command of their leader, instead of continuing in single file, they started to go abreast of one another. Not only that, they went without hurting trees and branches. Over sixty elephants moved in the shape of a crescent without noise and without damage. They spread out over a mile.

At the centre of the crescent was Sirdar. His trunk swung back and forth, up and down, to get the scent of danger. At the two ends of the crescent were two old bulls who had the longest experience of the jungle. They too swung their trunks every way to spy out the presence of man. Kumar walked behind the crowd to protect its rear from any attack. He stretched his trunk way behind to make sure that nothing was closing in on them.

Whatever each elephant found out, he telegraphed to the rest. That was done by a slight snort no louder than a man's whisper. Just picture to yourself more than three score elephants each one of them separated from the other by a wall of trees, sending wireless messages to the rest of the herd. The noise made was given forth in a key that no man could hear a foot away. Though it is called 'The warning snort' in reality it is no louder than the yawn of a waking child.

In the above fashion they moved about thirty minutes when Sirdar's nose smelt a hide-rope. He was in the act of picking up a twig from the ground when from under it came an odour of hide. He blew on the twig. Then he touched it again. Again the tip of his nostrils were repelled by the same odour as before. That confirmed his suspicion. So instead of investigating the trap with his trunk, he lifted his right fore-foot and with one toe of it—a mere horny plate—removed all the twigs that covered the thong. It was there! As a man is shaken when he sees a cobra at his feet, Sirdar trembled with the shock of his discovery. 'A trap! Shall I trumpet and sound the warning?'

That was his first thought. But instead, he put his foot forward again and played with the trap. As he worried it, it shrank in size. Slowly the loop became small as a man's wrist. Having found out the whole thing, he telegraphed to the herd: 'Snort, snort, snort.' That meant 'Tread carefully. Mark time.'

Then turning round he went to Kumar, touching the latter twice. That meant: 'Come with me; we must investigate.' Like clouds in the sky those two vast shapes vanished in the direction from which they had travelled the past hour. After running ten minutes they found what they wanted. Everywhere there was nothing but odour of man.

They flung their trunks to the right. Thence came the scent of man. To the left. The same odour greeted them. There! The air before them was deeply tainted with humanity.

When the presence of man becomes known, any pachyderm's first impulse is to run from it. But Sirdar and Kumar were so surprised that they could not move at all. Never in their lives had they experienced such a thing. The entire air before them seemed solid with humanity. What to do? Behind, Sirdar knew, were the traps. Before them was man—invisible, hence most sinister. What should he do for his followers? It was his fault. They had followed him into a terrible position. How to get them out of it?

Just then he heard something. He listened again. The same noise rose afar. Listen! Again the same noise; It was men talking! Terror, abject and relentless terror seizing them....

Sirdar would not run. He must find a way out of their present position. And that could not be done by flight.

Begging for a lead, 'Khan Khun Kun,' trumpeted the herd from behind. That was enough. They must hurry back to the frightened flock.

So they ran like two rabbits fleeing from a pack of hounds—noiselessly but very swiftly. They had to go far beyond the spot where they had left the herd, since the latter had moved away. That was bad. But what was worse was their renewed trumpeting. The noise of it was sending monkeys scurrying from tree to tree. Parrots in flocks shrieked and flew up like tattered and torn emerald banners. Boars grunted and dashed almost between the elephants' feet, and tigers suddenly roused from sleep roared in anger at them all, saying, 'Be quiet.'

At last when they had reached the herd they found four caught in four separate traps. Three bulls and a cow were trumpeting for their very life.

But that was nothing compared with what greeted Sirdar's eyes: a vast wooded structure—the real trap about a hundred yards ahead loomed like the very house of death.

If he told them what he and Kumar had found out, he knew there would be a terrible stampede that would lead them into the sinister wooden cage. The very mention of man would make them act like lunatics. Man to an elephant spells death.

What to do? What to do? The worst of all was happening now. The wind had changed. A faint scent of man was coming their way. Every hathi shivered as he caught the first whiff of that air. What to do? What to do?

'What must I do?' Sirdar hammered his own head with that question....

'Stampede. Stampede,' the herd had begun to mutter. Kumar whispered into his ear, 'Stampede.' Sirdar was so agitated that instead of stampeding into the wooden cage he ran the opposite way—a most helpful blunder. But before he went he ordered Kumar to bring up the rear.

The saying goes, 'Wherever the Chief flies the herd flies, too.' Though Sirdar's move was a blunder from the standpoint of the herd, yet it turned out differently. He did the thing that no average leader ever does. He told them to imitate his way of stampeding. They followed one, two, three, four ... after him. A magnificent single file they made as they ran at top speed, about fifteen to twenty miles an hour.

Before them the scent of man grew thicker, yet they pressed on. Here and there a hathi squealed. Sirdar trumpeted at him from ahead. Discipline, discipline, was his one thought. His cries lashed them into keeping form. Now the odour of man not only got thicker but along with it guns began to shoot. Hunter after hunter fired his rifle. The Chief stopped and lowered his head to receive the bullets. But lo! nothing stung him after the explosion. How strange! So he dashed ahead, resuming his march. Again—crack, crack of the rifles. Though he had stopped and lowered his head again no bullet hit him. This was very strange. Up till now whenever that noise took place, some elephants dropped dead. But on this occasion no one was hit. 'All the more reason to push forward,' Sirdar said to himself. No sooner said than done. He hurtled forward. Lo! there were two men running away towards a tree.

That made him see red. He charged at them. Fortunately the two ran up a tree in time. Otherwise they would have been trodden into mud. The flight of the men told the Chief that he had won. The bipeds were fleeing from him instead of he from them. Which proved to him that he was running in the right direction, so he pressed forward as before. On and on he ran, and the herd followed Sirdar out of the odour and sight of man. What a successful stampede!

Yet now he turned back alone to find out where Kumar was. Like a man entering a suffocating tube of poisonous gas, Sirdar returned to the man-infested jungle. Again began the crack, crack, crack of rifles and the yell of humans. Though he trembled with fear, yet he stood his ground. The hunters yelled, cracked the rifles anew yet no bullet struck him. Deafening yells broke out once more just ahead of him. Again the firearms made their noises. Sirdar stood still as if he were an elephant carved out of a rock.

What surprised him was that no bullet touched him. He stood as before and pondered. What was it all about?

Then and there he beheld Kumar coming to him leading two other elephants. The latter had broken the ropes of their traps and were running to safety guided by the bachelor. Poor Kumar! He was worn out with fatigue. He had helped to break the two thongs with his trunk. It felt sore and sick, sending stinging pain through his vast body.

Why did he not save the remaining members of the herd by breaking two more thongs? He had tried, but they were too strong for him. So he had to run with the two freed elephants before the men could shoot him to death, and because they were not hit by a single bullet they decided that the gods had protected them.

Alas! poor elephants, they did not know that the law of the land now permitted only the firing of blanks, the reason for which I will explain in the next chapter. This being a new law, the hathis understood nothing of it. They attributed their escape to a miracle. How like men are animals: men also very often attribute many good events of life to miracles. The only miraculous thing about such happenings is that we do not probe deeply enough to find their cause.

8

winter

After their latest escape the herd skirted the Ganges Delta and proceeded southwest. On their way they passed the Sunderbunds where Ghond the Hunter, the most famous tracker of the age, was the forest warden. Of course he loved animals in general and elephants in particular. But even Ghond was amazed at the health and discipline of Sirdar's followers. In fact he was so thrilled by them that he followed them two or three days from jungle to jungle just to feast his eyes on their beauty.

During their trek to the south, Sirdar and Kumar became more friendly than ever. They had always been kind to one another, but since their recent adventure they became inseparable cronies.

Now that the hunting season was on and men had come from England and America to winter and shoot in India, the elephants had to be careful about their movements. Their attitude of fear remained as before. They feared man because 'that animal with the gun' kills all living creatures.

Here the reader may wish to know the reason for the latest law prohibiting the shooting of hathis. India is the one place where elephants have been beasts of burden for centuries. Rarely have they been treated as game for sportsmen. With the coming of the Europeans, armed with high-power rifles, the destruction of hathis began. No one paid any attention to what might follow. Winter after winter rich Hindu princes and many European visitors shot in the jungle. They did not know what they were doing.

Suddenly towards the end of the nineteenth century it became evident to the wardens of the jungle that if not protected by law, the elephants as a species would run extinct in the not remote future. After a great deal of agitation the people and the government proclaimed elephant shooting to be a crime punishable by law.

Why should the elephant species be preserved? First of all, when tamed they make good draft animals. Next, since they do not breed well in captivity, they must be left alone in the wilds to breed and multiply. When they have grown in large quantities in the jungle the game wardens send the information to their superiors, who in time proclaim the year and the date of Kheddah, or capture in traps of elephants. Protection of wild hathis is essential to the life of the species as well as the life from which the renewal of stock of tamed pachyderms can be made. But Sirdar and his friends had not learnt of all this from the printed pages. To them the nearness of man meant death. Hence they travelled with care all winter. Every time men fired blank shots at them, the herd was sure that the shots had merely gone astray. That was all.

One day in January Kumar and his Chief had an adventure. The two of them, after leaving the herd to mill about in a safe place, had gone twenty miles further east and reached the edge of the town Chakradharpore, or the city of Chakradhar. There, from behind the last rows of the jungle-trees, they saw a tame female elephant carrying logs according to the orders of a man, the Mahout who sat on her neck. That sight distressed both of the wild ones. A feeling of anger and helplessness swept through their untamed hearts. Though the sight repelled them, yet they stood rooted to the spot and watched the work the young female was doing.

She in her turn felt frightened as she got wind of their presence. Her muscles quivered with excitement. Her effort at concealing from the Mahout her knowledge of the wild ones' presence was so intense that it succeeded. The biped on her back smelt no danger. He kept on tapping under her ear with his feet as he felt inclined to order her about. She obeyed him eagerly. Now we must explain why the tame elephant trembled. Her pleasure at seeing Kumar and Sirdar was just as great as her feat of them. If she were a male like them ehe would have been terrorised. For captive males are generally hated by the wild ones. The latter pitilessly charge those in bondage as soon as they see them. The reason for such conduct is quite explicable. As a free man hates the company of cowardly slaves, so free hathis have no mercy for the tame ones, particularly because it is the tame who bring gun-bearing men on their backs into the jungle to slaughter its innocent dwellers. That is generally the attitude of all wild creatures towards tamed hathis. But when wild males see a captive female, instead of anger, pity seizes their heart. In the present situation, Radha, the female, roused the friendliest feelings in Kumar and Sirdar. They watched her work the entire afternoon.

At last, with the sunset, she went with her Mahout, leaving behind two piles of logs many feet high as monuments to her slavery. Soon she carried her human burden out of sight into the town of Chakradhar.

None knows why Kumar and Sirdar, those two citizens of the forest, instead of going back to the herd remained at the edge of the small town and studied its life from a distance.

The short winter twilight drew veils of amber over the fields. Dark sapphire columns of smoke rose like prayers from the cottage chimneys. Herds of cattle came home from far-off meadows on the other side of the town. Night descended against the lilac horizon. Darkness fell—a rain of stillness plaining all the voices of day. Kumar listened to the silence of sundown while Sirdar held his trunk in a gesture of adoration to the last least flicker of sunlight. Hardly had his worship been over when the silver gongs of the town temples fretted the still air indicating that man, too, was adoring the Lord. What is the difference between the religions of beast and man? The former worship the visible god, the sun, while the latter prays to the God behind the visible. No matter who, he feels better for having performed an act of adoration.

With the coming of the dark the two bulls became very bold. They crept over the long meadows and reached the back yards of the town. The odour of humanity mingled with the odour of humanised beasts greeted their nostrils. Beasts in the wilderness have fainter odours than their tamed cousins, which is natural, for compared with the one, the other is sick. Living with man in complete security the animals that serve him become slow and take less exercise. That is why their skins look mangy when held next to those of their own species in nature. They give forth unhealthy odours which Kumar and Sirdar thought human. To them it was human-animal scent, hence most puzzling.

As they browsed about Chakradharpore, they frightened its dogs who ran indoors, and from behind their places of safety barked lustily. Their human masters now surmised that some wild wolves were abroad, which made them stay in their houses and gave the two hathis the run of the town. They looked through strange windows, put their trunks into fruit trees over brick walls, and placed their front feet against concrete houses in order to stand up on their hind legs and get a glimpse of humanity through lofty iron-barred windows. One old lady who saw the head of Sirdar etched against the risen moon screamed in terror. The hathis ran from that neighbourhood as if they had seen a hunter. She had succeeded in frightening them. Old ladies should not scream when wild elephants are about.

As they were trotting off, they suddenly caught a scent that, as it were, stung them. Standing very still, they sniffed the air again. Again the same odour: human-elephant! Sirdar grunted, as much as to say, it is the captive female of the afternoon. Drawn by an overpowering feeling of pity for her, they moved in her direction. And after fumbling through a couple of streets, and after frightening one more old lady, they reached the high-roofed pavilion where Radha stood, chained to two heavy tree stumps with iron shackles. She whinneyed almost like a horse at the very moment she felt the presence of the two wild males. Afraid to enter the pavilion and reluctant to go away, Kumar and Sirdar lingered under the eaves of the thatch-roof.

Slowly and shyly Radha put out her trunk and touched that of Sirdar. It sent an electric shock of surprise through him. After a few minutes' hesitation he put forth his trunk and felt one of her forelegs down to the ankle where the cold links of the iron chain lay like a coiled viper. The feel of it brought back to his mind the years and incidents of his boyhood when he too slaved for man with his own mother. The thumping of human heels against his ear-drum, the sharp dig of the ankus and many other cruel memories rushed upon him. A feeling of irresistible pain seized his brain. In his anguish he strove to break Radha's chain. Alas! of no avail. The iron was young and the links too strong. Kumar, who was an expert at breaking thongs and traps, tried to break the chain that bound Radha's hind foot. All his cunning and strength failed to weaken a single link. Now he thought of smashing the tree-stumps to which the chain was fastened. Were they over five feet high that could be done by walking backwards against them. But stumps that were hardly three feet in height and two in diameter grazed his knees severely each time Kumar tried to walk them out of existence.

Finding all their efforts fruitless the two bulls stopped to take counsel. Just then the town roosters crowed dawn. Not only that, the ground of the town began to shake slightly. That told its tale. Sirdar, leading Kumar, ran from the pavilion as fast as he could go. The rate of their speed must have been twenty miles an hour. Hardly had they gone several hundred yards when Sirdar saw the entire herd walking towards the town like a horde of monsters. They were coming to try and rescue their leader who, they imagined, had been trapped by the town-folk. And you never heard such squeals of pleasure and trumpeting as when Sirdar and Kumar joined them.

The whole town was frightened out of its sleep. Men and women ran upstairs to their roofs to find out the source of such calamitous cries. What they saw they could not believe. In fact the next day when people narrated their experience to those who had slept through the night, they were called liars. 'Bosh, you did not see a hundred elephants run about here. Why, the last time wild elephants that were seen here was before the railroad came in 1850. Nonsense, you did not see elephants, you dreamt of them in your sleep.'

Later in the day all those doubting humans had to eat their own words when they saw innumerable footprints of hathis on their fields and pastures.

'Unbelievable,' they exclaimed in unison. But what followed proved still more unbelievable. During the afternoon when the Mahout had done his work preparatory to going home with his beast of burden, he got off Radha's back in order to inspect from the ground the two extra piles of logs that she had amassed. In India logging is done in this way: after the specially selected trees have been cut, the wood-cutters leave it to the Mahout to have the timber dragged out of the jungle to its edge with the help of his elephant. After that, ox-carts fetch the logs to the nearby towns. But it is the duty of the Mahout to see to it that all the logs are arranged symmetrically by his charge. So this particular afternoon in order to make quite sure that Radha had done her work well, he inspected the results of her efforts. He went around each separate pile and whistled to his own satisfaction.

While he was whistling he suddenly felt something pull the turban off his head. He turned to see who had dared to insult him thus. For in India to unturban a stranger is tantamount to striking him in the face. So the terribly angry Mahout looked over his shoulder for his enemy. Then what he saw made him turn green with terror! A wild elephant was unravelling the folds of his turban, while another was walking off with Radha into the jungle. Between him and the others stood Kumar, still playing with his turban. The Mahout leapt to his right and ran out of the reach of Kumar's trunk. Had he stood still longer, Kumar would have killed him. Now seeing the man run, he realized that the turban was not the man. That made him so angry that he gave chase. Fortunately the Mahout was a skilled elephant hunter. He ran around the piles of wood, thus giving the tusker a zig-zag path to follow. Of course the elephant's small eyes lost sight of him behind one of the timber-piles. And just when Kumar turned away from him, the Mahout ran into the jungle. Though he ran bare-footed on the grass, the sound of it, no louder than a mouse creeping across a cement floor, reached the ear of his foe whose sensitive hathi-hearing missed nothing. Again Kumar was in mad pursuit. He must have attained a very high speed. Had not the Mahout reached a plane-tree and dodged behind it, then around another, while the elephant was still smelling round the first one, the poor fellow would have been trampled into pulp. Now he pursued a zig-zag course in between a score of trees before he dared climb up a good sal whose top he reached a few minutes before Kumar got there. But since the hathi could not see him above his own head, he was at a loss what to do. Just then another elephant came and touched him from behind. That meant, 'Sirdar has reached the herd with Radha, whom you two came to rescue; now we are waiting for you to join us. The Chief orders you to come.' No sooner heard than done. Kumar gave up looking for the Mahout and vanished into the forest with his friend.

After half an hour more when the jungle was quite dark the Mahout got down onto the ground and ran across the fields to his home in the town. That night when he told the people assembled in the town temple what had happened to him, instead of sympathy he got only a scolding. A village elder called him, 'Oh, thou brainless half-brother of a mule, dost thou not know that it costs money to buy elephants?' Another castigated him thus: 'Oh, thou beardless son of an earthworm, Oh, father of a hundred baboons.' So on and on for an hour. Such is the life of a Mahout. If he preserves his hathi he is admired; if he loses it he is cursed. What a life!

9

accepted by the herd

It was one thing to rescue the young female from captivity but quite another thing to get her accepted by the herd. Every one save Kumar and Sirdar resented her presence. They did not like Radha's peculiarity, which was to give out not only the odour of sickness, but also of man. That she was not sick was quite clear, but living as she had done for years under man's rule had made her muscles slack from lack of exercise. Her skin, because of a bad circulation of blood, was poor, too. It lacked the ebony polish of the wild hathis. They rarely rest more than two hours at a time. They move always. But Radha had not done much exercising during all the nights she spent in civilization, which had apparently injured her health. Besides the odour of humans there clung to her other marks of civilization. It seemed as if she was tattooed by man, and every wild beast could read the marks by looking at her.

It was fortunate that Kumar and Sirdar, her sponsors, were not negligible members of their group, so that when they claimed admission for her into their family it was not refused then and there. Instead, a provisional arrangement was arrived at. She was permitted to go wherever the herd went, but she was not allotted a place in it, either. She had to march behind or beside the others as best she could. She had no station nor duties to perform. Though their treatment of her seemed heartless, it was surely better than being a slave under Mahout, her human master. Moreover, there is no nobler way devised by other species for the accommodation of immigrants. Take, for example, newcomers to America: they have to pass medical and other immigration examinations before they are admitted to the country and even after their entry, it takes most of them a long time before they can make friends with representative native Americans.

Radha was an immigrant from the slavedom of man to the free life of the jungle. That she was accepted there at all was a mark of great favour. But as time passed and as she lost all the marks and taints of servitude, she became more and more a part of the flock. By the time July had come and gone she was assigned a place in the herd. Now she had her stations and duties. She had to give and receive signals. She stood her ground in moments of crisis, and passed the final test of a genuine member of the family when she risked her life to save that of others.

This took place in the month of Agrahyana, September. Agrahyana if pronounced Agrariana will give one the real sense of the word. It is the month of harvest. During its thirty days 'agriculture' reaches its climax. Over the whole Ganges valley the harvest floats like a battle-flag of gold. Heavy kine throbbing with fat draw their silken flanks through the grain-fields. All nature puts on abundance for dress. The Ganges itself, full from shore to shore, runs swiftly like a thousand tawny lions.

At that time even the most well-disciplined herd of elephants, despite all warning, break the command of their elders and go into the grain-fields and eat up the crops. That is what happened to Sirdar's crowd. He and Kumar had left them milling about in a thin forest near the valley where evening descended, drawing after it veils of flaming gold.

It was the night of the harvest moon. Sirdar and Kumar went into the deeper jungle with the intention of playing and swimming all night in the waters of a lake. The others preferred to stay where they were and enjoy the evening. Soon the dawning of the moon made the east honey-coloured. It hurled on their heads and backs spears of silver light. They lifted their trunks as if to draw the cool fire of the risen moon into their nostrils like water.

A monkey finding sleep out of the question looked down from a high bough. What he saw made him jump with excitement. Under the touch of the magic of night he too was exceeding all caution. Softly he slid down from branch to branch till he was close enough to see everything in detail. The elephants were dancing. Not one or two, but a whole herd, skipping and scurrying in a circle. What a sight! Generally the Hanus, the monkeys, chatter a great deal. But the sight of hathis dancing was marvellous enough to rob him of his speech. He shivered in joy as he saw huge tuskers touch trunks and pass each other in serried circles. Circle within circle spun and swam under his eyes. This was a veritable miracle—the most memorable night of his life. No wonder it made the monkey speechless.

Just then he smelt panther above. As he looked up he saw two green eyes blazing down on him. Their gaze was like the bolt of death. The panther could reach out a paw and break his skull. What was he to do? What could he do? Below him a forest of elephant feet was hammering the earth into mud-oozing vegetable juice. If he leaped on to the ground he would be trampled into mud in no time. And above him the two green eyes glowed over the steaming breath of the black cat. 'G r r r,' growled the enemy. The sound pierced into his stupid mind like a goad. Without thinking twice, the monkey leaped forward. The cat, too, leaped. But the monkey landed on the neck of a hathi where he clung desperately. The elephant at once reared and trumpeted. The confusion that followed engulfed the panther who had missed both monkey and elephant and disappeared between the dancing feet. In no time he was trampled into pulp.

But that was enough to break the spell of their pleasure. The herd moved away from the place where the killer had been trodden to death. The monkey, finding himself safe, jumped off the elephant's neck and vanished up a tree. His life had been saved by Radha.

But that was not the only act of mercy she performed that night. An hour or so later, unable to sleep and possessed by the magic of the moon, the herd decided to eat the grain from the cultivated fields. In spite of all the rules against such a procedure, they stealthily moved towards the open country. By midnight they reached the hay-cocks that stood in the meadows. Unable to resist, the elephants set about to feast upon them. But Radha, who knew man better than they, hung back. She went around to the other side of the hay-cocks, and searched. There she found ripe bananas lying here and there. This was most unusual. She ate a few of them, and looked about, but still wondered how bananas could grow in the grass. Suddenly, she knew not why, she looked over the heads of the elephants,

Lo! there were lights behind them. Ah! beaters! She knew them. They had been closing in upon the whole herd. There was no doubt now that they were in the front of a Kheddah.

Any inexperienced wild elephant would have been frightened out of its wits. The sight of torches, which symbolizes forest fire, produces abject fear in most young wild animals. But Radha, who had lived with man long, was used to the sight of fire of all kinds. So she stood and watched, trying to make out the nature and extent of the present danger. She could not begin to fathom the depth of the situation. These men had followed the herd for days and had noticed the absence of Kumar and Sirdar from the rest this night. Now that the group was leaderless the beaters decided to close in upon them.

Seeing the hathis in the grain-fields, they lighted their torches in order to frighten the herd into the open where Kheddah pits had been dug. And all the holes in the ground were covered with leaves, branches and fruits. An elephant could reach out and lift the fruits with his trunk and eat them. But were he to walk nearer he would step through a thin cover of leaves and branches into a pit many feet deep. Once there he would have to depend on human beings to pull him out. Elephants can do many things but they cannot jump out of pits. And frightened, the herd would run and fall into the pits. Radha instinctively knew this danger.

The trouble that threatened them now began to be felt by half a dozen or more elephants. The wind was bringing down to them the scent of the torches. Every second the faint odour of burnt oil and rags grew more perceptible than before. Panic, like a vise, seized the first six. Then through them it spread into the rest of the herd. It was terrible. Imagine about sixty elephants trembling with terror. A ghastly sense of indecision made them go round and round the hay-cocks like a blind man's procession. Radha was the least frightened of all. She was not in the moving circle of fear and therefore she could keep her head. But the sight before her was so distressing that, unable to bear it any longer, she dashed away at a tremendous pace in a line parallel to the torches and the pits, trumpeting shrilly 'Follow me, follow me to safety.' In this direction only it happened that the torches had not yet circled down and closed her exit. Her decision communicated itself to the others. Since they had no time to think out a plan of action of their own, they imitated whatever she did. One after the other trumpeted and ran, treading in her footsteps. The torch-bearers seeing their prey escape them, fired blank shots. They also set off sticks of dynamite. A terrific detonation filled the air. But that, instead of driving the herd into the pits, made the elephants follow the direction already taken. In ten more minutes all the noise had lost itself in the silence of the sky whence the moon poured her magic with silver hands.

After describing a curve of some miles, the elephants reached the jungle in a roundabout way. They were so humiliated by their own stupid behaviour that whatever was left of the night they spent quietly like a pack of whipped dogs.

Soon Kumar and Sirdar returned. They were glad to learn of Radha's exploit, but they reprimanded the herd for breach of discipline. They now settled Radha's position in the family: She was not only accepted but honoured by all. Any human being looking at them would have thought that nothing new had arisen in their midst. Men cannot easily believe that animals too honour their great. But, in fact, wherever animals gather, they select leaders and obey them, which proves that though they do not clap hands and send cablegrams, all of God's creatures give expression to gratitude and admiration in their own peculiar way. This is exactly what the herd did to Radha when they realized that it was she who had led them out of their great trouble.

10

love and marriage

There was one particular elephant who was fonder of Radha than the rest—it was Sirdar. After her masterly act of leadership Sirdar paid marked and increasing attention to her. Of course between her and himself lay a common bond: their knowledge of man and civilization. The sharing of such a secret drew them together. From now on, Kumar and Sirdar always took Radha with them if they went on any excursion of their own. Thus another winter passed, while they went as far south as the Eastern Ghat Hills of Madras. But by the first of March it grew so hot there that the herd started for the cool region of the Himalayas.

In the north the *shishim* were bursting their emerald buds; the *dhak* flowers stretched out their petals like fingers of flame, and the *sandans* shed their lilac glow between corrugated brown bark and tiny tender leaves. Still further north the cherries spread delicate splendour and the almonds wrought a gem-like charm against the white hills. The swallows flew through the moonlight from Ceylon to the Himalayas, swifts roamed the turquoise heavens at all hours, and the wild pigeons returned to build their nests on the ledges of Hudro, the Indian Niagara Falls. At last the humming birds reached Kashmir, placing their official seal on the wax of Spring.

But before going to that Paradise on earth, the Valleys of Khashmeer (as it should be pronounced), we must tarry with Sirdar and his followers at Horda where the Subarnarekha—the thread of gold—falls in a steady tide of topaz into deep abysses of rocks studded with green-black trees. There the sun glints the falls with stinging scarlet as he bounds, at dawn, over 'the eastern hills like a stallion of fire.'

It took the hathis all of March to reach the Hudro. They stood at the foot of the falls and watched the water thunder down more than four hundred and thirty feet. But the awe and wonder of that spectacle did not thrill the elephants as much as the sight of wild blue pigeons who flew in and out of their nests in the rock through the dazzling streams of topaz. How could they do it without being drowned?

After circling round the Hudro, the herd moved further north. Another month's march brought them to the forests of Kashmir where the battle for mates was to be staged. At this particular mating season the herd was having a slight discussion as to the wisdom of the Chief's choice of a wife. A Chief may order his followers to do his bidding in everything save to accept his sweetheart. The female that he loves must be approved by the herd before she and her children may become members of it.

That Sirdar would choose Radha for his mate was taken for granted, for in time their gratitude to both of them overcame all of their objections to the marriage. But still there remained one more obstacle in Sirdar's path. This proved to be most serious.

One day while Kumar and Sirdar were wandering by themselves on the shore of a lake in the direction of Dal, Sirdar was rudely told by his friend that he too was in love with Radha. This stunned the Chief. His best friend in love with Radha. What a situation! How was he to straighten the matter out?

It is the code of honour among elephants that a Chief who sacrifices everything for his herd should not give up his mate to anyone without fighting. In the history of the hathis, no male relinquishes his chosen cow without being worsted in battle. Sirdar was left no other choice in the matter. In the meantime Radha, seeing what was going to happen, discreetly withdrew under the trees and nibbled twigs and saplings.

While she was busy eating leaves like sugar candy, the two males challenged each other loudly, then set to fighting. The glens of Kashmir echoed with their trumpeting, while from nowhere a flock of monkeys, who always enjoy a fight, came to witness the lovers' battle. They sat spell-bound and quiet as mice while the elephants made the earth tremble under their feet, and the heavens shake with their bellowing.

At first matters fared badly with Sirdar. Kumar, who had done more fighting than the Chief, knew better than to strike gently. He ripped the latter's side open with a terrific thrust and sidelong pull of his sharp tusks. Fortunately the wound was not deep, only long. But it electrified Sirdar. The flow of blood and the sharp pain made him forget Kumar's identity. Now he fought as one fights an unknown opponent. Without any delay he lowered his head and lunged under Kumar's chest. But the bachelor was too adroit. He dashed off at a tangent clear out of his leader's range, then, turning round, he sought to get at his rear. Sirdar had stayed the momentum of his first thrust and turned half-way about.

So instead of the rear, it was his already lacerated side that got the full force of Kumar's attack. It was a most nerve-racking blow, and made him dizzy. Even the monkeys above chattered in pain at the sight of his suffering. Now a genuine fury seized him. It made his mind act coolly, though his muscles became tense like a python about to strike. Ere Kumar had disengaged his tusks from his flank, Sirdar flung his trunk around his neck and throat and began to throttle him. As Kumar jerked his tusks to get them out of his victim's body, one of them broke as easily as a reed broken by a shepherd. This smote dismay into his heart, and the entire weight of Sirdar's body pulling his neck and squeezing his throat began to tell. Slowly but steadily he sank, while he flung his trunk about to grip the throat of his adversary. But Sirdar's head being under his own chin, he could not get much leverage, and somehow instead of the latter's throat his trunk coiled around his adversary's lower lip and tusks. In a few minutes he began to suffocate. Then Kumar quickly bore his entire weight down on Sirdar's head and produced the desired result. The trunk around his own neck relaxed.

But then Kumar did something stupid. He tried to disengage his own trunk in order to grip the throat of his foe with it and instantly the Chief butted ahead with his tusks and buried them deep in Kumar's chest. The latter reared on his hind legs in order to free himself from them, but too late. Sirdar too had reared and kept going deeper, nearing the poor fellow's heart. There was nothing for Kumar to do now but to die fighting. Standing on his hind legs he lashed his rival's eyes with his trunk. One, two, three—on eyes and ears the blows fell. Sirdar, whose trunk was in his mouth, could not bring it out in time to parry those dizzying blows. Blow after blow made him sick with confusion. Instead of one Kumar, he saw ten elephants fighting him. At last his resistance gave out. With one long, hard backward pull, he drew out his tusks from Kumar's chest. Blood ran like a river from the latter's mouth and breast. Frightened and beaten, he dashed out of sight. Though victorious, the Chief felt sick almost to death. He knelt down and rested his tusks on the ground. It seemed as though he would die. Soon the sun fell, the monkeys slunk away from the tree-tops, and insects set up their orchestration of stabbing sounds. Slowly Radha came from behind the trees, and passed her trunk over his back. Then she put her trunk under his tusks and helped to raise him to his feet. Slowly the two walked to the herd in order to proclaim that they were going to be married.

It took Sirdar nearly a month to regain his normal health. During that time and until July, he and Radha wandered by themselves. It was the happiest period of their lives. After the rain had fallen, they rejoined the herd in the eastern Jumna valley, about three hundred miles southeast of Allahabad.

What happened to Kumar? He became a Rogue, a solitary wandering bachelor. He never married anyone. There are many Rogues like him. They are ill-tempered males who live alone and terrorise men and beasts within a radius of miles of their jungle home.

Kumar did what all Rogues do. He had been seen

in the jungles of Gharwal recently, still alone and still acting like a crotchety bachelor. Though he is over seventy-nine years old he has never since looked upon a female elephant. Once he got a glimpse of the old herd led by Sirdar and saw Radha. But instead of giving any signs to his old friends, the heart-sick Rogue plunged into a deep ravine and hid till they had all passed beyond sight, sound and scent.

11

bahadur, son of sirdar

About two years after their marriage, Bahadur the Brave, the son of Sirdar, was born. At his birth his weight was one hundred and eight pounds, and his height nearly three feet. He looked grey at first, but grew dark rapidly.

The first day of his life Bahadur spent mostly in a sitting posture. The greater part of the second day he spent on his feet. Before the fourth day was over, he was able to walk a great deal. This is very different from the behaviour of human infants of the same age. Other animals too are not as strong at birth as hathis. A new-born heifer or a steer within a week of its birth cannot spend seven to nine hours a day on its feet, but an elephant can. He has one advantage over all the land animals of his age. He takes a year more than they before he is born. The tiger cubs are born only a few months old. Bison calves do not differ much from this. But an elephant, the moment he arrives on earth, is at least twenty-one months old. He is better formed than the others; he is stronger than the others in every respect, and that is why he can spend hours on his feet in such a short time after his birth.

Moreover, in order to get milk, he has to reach the udders of his mother, which he can do only by standing up. Since the infant wills to live, he must have food, and since he needs a lot of it he has to stand a long time.

Next, we must never forget that generally wild hathis walk, stand still, and sleep on their feet. Only a few are ever seen seated on the ground. In fact not a single member of Sirdar's herd, after he was three years old, had ever knelt or lain on the ground for the purpose of resting. If they knelt down, in adult life, it was only to reach the ground in order to dig up something with their tusks, and that position they maintained for a very short time. Unless he is very young, it is natural for an elephant to be on his feet day and night.

Bahadur spent all his waking hours on his feet. Only during three hours of rest in the middle of the day and eight hours of sleep at night he lay down between the legs of one of his parents, both of whom spent those hours standing still. Though both of them dozed, they rarely slept, while their son slumbered peacefully. This proves that animals, too, sacrifice themselves for their young as men and women do.

From this point let us imagine ourselves as hathis, so that we can hear from Sirdar himself the story of Bahadur's upbringing. It is very easy for him to talk about his gifted son, for elephant fathers do not hesitate to display their pride and pleasure in their offspring. Truth to tell, they really enjoy talking about their calves. In this respect some men have a great deal to learn from dumb beasts.

'After saluting the gods of the elephants, after thanking them for giving me a noble son, I shall tell you of the art of bringing up my eldest born, Bahadur. I hope you will understand my elephant-language all the way through.

'At the very outset let me tell you that both Radha and I were more than painstaking about his welfare. Every time he sneezed we jumped with panic. We were afraid he had whooping-cough or pneumonia. It is not at all pleasant for a baby elephant to whoop all night.

'However, all our fears proved baseless, for Bahadur grew up to be a sturdy and intelligent fellow. But since habits formed within the first few years of a person's life make up the sum total of his character, we took extra pains in this regard with Bahadur. He rested regularly in the afternoons and slept soundly eight hours of the night. He had to do all this for his own good, for he who cultivates repose and sleeps as he should, grows stronger and braver than the youngsters who do not.

'Next to acquiring regular habits, came learning. In order to achieve this end, the day he was a month old we travelled by easy stages towards our herd. In the lives of elephants the instinct to be with the herd is developed early, and the greater part of the calf's education is given him in the herd. Since the group saves the individual in times of peril, he should be initiated into group life very early. He should not become a blind follower of the herd, but if he is to grow into one of its intelligent members, the sooner he studies it and lives with it the better he will like its virtues and dislike its weaknesses. In bringing up the young, love of strength and beauty should be made a part of their nature. The surest way of doing that is to form the habit of courage, repose and intelligence. Since character is but the sum total of a person's habits, every youngster should build it by means of the latter.

'On reaching our herd we were welcomed with great warmth. Very gentle and most pleasant calls filled the air. Trunk met trunk in gestures of friendliness. With such a kind group to welcome us, Radha and I were very happy. Hardly had we finished greeting one another when our child disappeared among a crowd of other children whose parents too had rejoined the herd recently. All-told there were about half a dozen youngsters of Bahadur's age. Now that Spring was upon us, we marched northwards in the direction of Mount Everest. Suddenly like the thrust of a dagger came into my memory the face of Kumar, my old friend. It was in his company that I first saw the snow petals of the Everest peaks open like a flower and the morning star vanish into its opal heart.

'Hardly had I lost myself in the sad thoughts of Kumar when Ajit, the ninety-nine-year-old deputy leader who had been leading the herd in my absence, stood for orders. His face beamed with approval of my son Bahadur. We decided that Ajit should bring up the rear of the herd. Radha must travel in front of him, and before her should march Bahadur, so that the lad's rear might be protected first by his mother and then by the wisest elephant of all. This arrangement was made, so that the Chief should not have his wife and child near him, lest the thought of their safety trouble him so greatly that he jeopardise the rest of the herd. Now after an absence of two months, I stood at the head and led the procession of my friends and family.'

12

sirdar continues

'The first night we halted in the delta of the Ganges, the Sundarbans, whose jungles are full of tigers and leopards, and its streams packed with crocodiles. The water was salty, and undrinkable. So we had to dig with our feet in certain places and drink from springs that were a few inches below the earth's surface.

'Bahadur's sleeping arrangements had to be quite new this time. He was obliged to sleep in a group with the other babies. Around them we placed, in the form of a ring, all the youngsters below ten. Next to them stood all the mothers of the flock in a circle; these we hemmed in and protected with a ring of boys below thirty years of age, and last of all came the ring made by the adults of the herd standing nose to tail. After having seen to this and taking my place in the ring of the big male elephants, I ordered all to sleep soundly.

Nothing untoward happened till sunrise when two hungry tigers circled around us a few times, examining our formation. Soon they tired of this and went off in quest of other things.

'We did not keep this formation during the rest hour of the day; instead, the parents, both male and female, watched over their respective children. Sometimes two or three families grouped together and went off by themselves. Generally the children would sleep all in a bunch while the parents stood silent like ebony walls around them. Elephants keep very quiet, not only during the rest hours of infants but most of the time. This is probably due to our size. Normally we expose so much of ourselves to danger that, in order to keep adequate watch over our own safety, we have to listen, look and smell with the utmost stillness. Stillness is our normal environment no matter where we are. Any disturbed surroundings are uncongenial to us.

'After they have had their rest, the children play with their own parents. This rule was rarely broken during the first twelve months of a calf's life. After all, the little fellows could not march all morning and all afternoon without some hours of real play. We generally took Bahadur with us and played with him. But one afternoon the parents decided to teach the youngsters how to swim. By this time Bahadur was about three months old. Each child stood between his father and mother, and all of them waited on the river bank for a signal from me. But I could not order them to plunge in without making sure that not only the jungle behind us was safe but also that the water before us was uninhabited by crocodiles and sharks. So I put my trunk into it and took a little water, which I tasted with my tongue. Since it was not salty I decided that there could be no sharks in it. Then, in order to be perfectly sure that there were no crocodiles under the surface lurking to attack us, I buried half of my trunk into its depth and waited. Since no animal bit my nose, though I held it as long as I could, I decided it was safe. Even then the mothers would not let the children go in. So we, the males, swam in a crescent shape half-way across. Elephants do that in order to clear a few yards of water from all animals. When the water-dwellers see such vast shapes plough their world with so many legs, they leave their place to us without much ado. After that last gesture of precaution, we called our wives and children to join us. The infants refused to budge. They preferred the shore to the swim.

'Now each father had to go up and coax his child to come down. Our son refused to put a foot off the ground. What were we to do? At last I told him that we were going across the river. This frightened him all the more. Then I pointed to his mother who was floating in the water, which meant that all elephants float. They never drown. Hathis are too fat to sink anywhere. But

Bahadur proved obdurate. So his mother came half-way up the shore and put her trunk around him. In the meantime all the other parents had coaxed their infants off the ground. Seeing them floating and as Radha began to pull him, I pushed Bahadur from behind. In an instant he was in the river. I jumped after him. He tried to balance himself by wriggling his legs, but that made him roll over. I had to put my trunk around his and keep him from putting it into the water. Now he floated evenly and in a few minutes I let go of his trunk but instead of holding it up, he let it sink. In a flash Radha lowered her own and pulled it up. The instant it emerged out burst a veritable fountain of water accompanied by trumpeting.

'Again after floating a while, his mother let go his nose. This time too he let it sink. I had to push mine after it, swiftly bringing both of them again into the air. This time he and I both shot out a lot of water. My head fairly ached with pain and confusion. I must say that Bahadur was not a complete duffer, for the third time his nose was released he kept it erect above the water, and thus we taught him how to float in the river. The next day he learned to use his feet properly, and, lo! before the week was out, he was fording rivers with the utmost ease.

'Next to conquest of water, the thing that an elephant should know is the conquest of the air. I mean by that that a calf, before he is a year old, should be able to tell by the odour in the atmosphere what animal is passing him.

'In the beginning we taught him to divide the odours into two classes—one of the vegetarian, the other of the meat-eating beasts. Next, we taught him to distinguish cats from dogs as the two distinct types of killers. He learned also to distinguish wolves from wild dogs, and leopards from tigers. All this took time to learn. But before he was two years old, Bahadur knew all that there was to know from us about the scent of an animal.

'The greatest danger that he ever ran into was when we were teaching him to recognize wolves, leopards, and the cobra. He was almost devoured by wolves one day. It was during the second rainy season of his life. Though it was the season for great downpours, no rain had fallen till July. The whole world was stricken with drought. Brooks dried as fast as a water-drop disappears in sandhills. Rivers grew thin as an elephant's tail, then stopped running. Trees whose roots did not go deep died in a short time. Grass and reeds throbbed with heat like yellow wastes. Stung by thirst and hunger, we proceeded towards the mouth of the Ganges where there was at least the sea.

'But it is the moral law of the jungle that when the drought comes all the animals, whether killers or prey, cease hunting and hurting one another. In the face of a common danger such as drought or flood, the animals do not struggle for existence. They co-operate and foes and friends help each other to escape from the zone of danger.

'We made sure, from the birds who spread the news, that this calamity of drought was upon us. They, being used to flying great distances, can tell how far-reaching troubles can be. Then after they spread the bad news, the elephants who travel nearly as far, for they wander day and night, give the call. Between the birds and the hathis the people who catch the news from below and above are the monkeys. They love to bring and broadcast news. Now all of them, puffed up with self-importance, ran from tree to tree, jabbering and screaming: "Arise, awake, run before you die of thirst." But the idiots did not tell people which way to run. That is why a general stampede began. It looked as if the whole jungle was to run in all directions at once. The screams of terrified beasts grew horrible. The din of it froze one's hearing. Suddenly a cry lashed the air. It slashed and smashed the other sounds and made them still. "Bonka, bonok, bawn," bellowed the wild buffaloes. They alone had the nose for the water; they were shouting for us to follow their lead to the sea. Why is it that the cows are more fitted to find water than any other animal? Of course the birds are the best guide to any place far off, but they cannot tell by the odour of the soil whether there is water under it. Both the bovine and the hathi races can do that. Birds see. We smell. Since their figures of speech are in terms of eight, we do not grasp them.

'Hence during our present search for water, the buffaloes had to lead. Their leadership we could understand, for they used their nostrils like the rest of us. Close behind them followed the tigers and leopards. Next went all the hathis. This was a good precaution, for in case the buffaloes missed out, our trunks might find water. After us were the antelopes, deer, bears, dogs and many other tribes. Thus we marched in the utmost friendliness. We had the monkeys and birds overhead. They, too, kept on moving like the rest, but as one might foresee, many of the monkeys abandoned the quest after several days. I am told that they perished of the drought. Of all races the Hanumans are most changeable, and that is the reason of their suffering and misery.

'After a week's journey we reached a river at least half-full of water. All the animals drank together of its water, clean as the eye of a bird. Oh! what a relief! Every species was filled with joy. After drinking, bathing began. Animal after animal wallowed in the broad shallow river in the very open. No fear of kind showed itself amongst us. The past few days' friendly intercourse had erased all memories of fear and hate from our hearts.

'Alas! no noble emotion prevails long amongst mortals. It was a pack of wolves who rekindled the flame of slaughter toward sundown that day. While Radha, Bahadur and I were eating a few twigs from the neighbouring trees, suddenly we heard the bark of distress from a Sambur, big deer. We looked in vain for him. No matter which way we looked we could get no more sound nor scent of him. My nose told me nothing for a minute or so; Radha too could not tell a thing. But Bahadur's young and powerful nostrils told him that a dog or two were drawing nearer. Since he feared no dogs, he went forward in their direction. We followed him at a distance.

'No sooner had he taken a dozen more steps than a Sambur, red and flaming with sweat, leapt past us. Bahadur trumpeted, saying he smelt more dog. Since dog meant no danger to him, we walked on without haste. We were bent on eating a few more twigs. Then came a ghastly call for help from our son. We ran as fast as we could, but we had to pass between trees which his small body had cleared easily. That took some time. In the meanwhile the trumpets of the boy were drowned by a horrible yell of wolves. Radha, urged by her mother love, smashed half a dozen trees with her head as she flung herself headlong. I followed fast. It seemed as if years had passed before we could reach the howling wolves. There, there…what I saw almost froze my blood. Our only son running in a circle before a pack of ravenous howling brutes. They had closed in upon him. "In one more wink of my eye they will be upon him," I thought. Radha, with upraised trunk, shrilly shouting, ran at them. Her cries did not stop them, but the boy had heard her voice. It nerved him. Instead of running about aimlessly he stopped and trumpeted a challenge. That roar—the roar of a master—held his pursuers at bay for several seconds.

'Now, in answer to him, I trumpeted back. It was my master call; its pitch makes the whole jungle listen. The wolves turned their heads and instantly took fright. For, behold! Radha was upon them. Her feet kicked them about like pebbles. With a dozen more kicks she cleared a path through them to her son's side. Now the wolves leaped and snapped at her. One of them tore at her trunk. The very sight of it hurled me forward faster. Of course they had been so busy with her that they had not seen me approaching. Like a hill falling with the softness of a sigh but swift as a thunderbolt, I came upon them. I smashed into them with all my might. My four tons trampled dozens to death, yet there were more wolves to kill. They poured at us from every direction. Now I brought my trunk into action; every time one of them leaped in the air, I broke his back with one blow. I swung my nose with as much effect as if it were a hammer. Skulls cracked, ribs broke, and bones were crushed under our feet like river reeds. And still they attacked. Panting, groaning and kicking, I ran round to the exposed side of Bahadur. Seeing that both of his flanks were protected he stopped trumpeting. Now he too fought. With his little feet he stepped on those who, though wounded refused to run away. Thus we fought, three to a hundred, ere those dogs would turn tail. At last, after what seemed a long long year of wolf-slaughtering, we found several scores of them fleeing for their lives.

'That gave us too a chance to flee the place. It is not pleasant to kill or to inhale the odour of blood. It is sickening. No elephant loves carnage of any kind. Unlike human beings, we do not like waging wars. We rushed to the river to wash off all the stains of it from our body. While washing in the cool flood, Bahadur avowed that he would never mistake the odour of wolf for that of mere dogs, for mistakes like that are very costly.

'Ho! I can hear the question that is rising in your thought. Let me answer it. I can read your mind. You are saying: "How do odours seem to him?" Well, each odour strikes us differently. For instance, elephants smell vegetarian beasts only very faintly. Buffaloes, stags, and sheep smell alike: only in the case of the sheep the odour is very heavy. By the way, you can separate those who eat vegetables from the killers without any trouble. All meat-eating animals smell like dead things. Their odour is not only heavy but foul. To us, hathis, meat-eaters are diseased if not deadly.

'Of the meat-eaters the cats are different from the dogs. The former generally eat only what they kill, but the latter eat what is already dead or killed by another. They smell more foul than the tiger and the leopard. Of all the dogs the hyena is easy to recognize by his scent, for he eats nothing but carrion. Dogs and wolves eat less carrion than hyenas, but dogs eat more of it than wolves. That is how one can distinguish the one from the other. To me a dog smells like a rat, and a wolf more like a weasel. Two odours that you cannot distinguish from each other are those of tigers and leopards. They are difficult to separate. Young tigers are easy to tell for they never eat carrion. Leopards eat carrion occasionally, but so do old tigers, who, owing to failing strength, do not always succeed in making a kill. So they go about and rob small packs of wolves, cheetahs and young panthers of their prey. If a panther hides his victim anywhere on the ground, the old tigers steal and eat it up. But that only complicates a hathis problem of smelling one kind of cat apart from another. If a young elephant ever brags that he can always distinguish a leopard from a tiger by its odour, be sure that youth is telling a tall story. Don't trust what he has to say. On the contrary you can put your faith in any member of our race who prides himself on telling dogs apart from cats. That we can do most successfully. Even though they eat carrion, the cats lick themselves, and sometimes they swim in the river and wash themselves clean. Their odour is fresher than the dogs', who are dirtier; they eat corpses in any stage of decay, and most of the time they smell to Heaven. Their odour is unmistakable.

'Here let me say in conclusion that this particular fight with the wolves after our escape from the drought- smitten region taught our son Bahadur not to be too sure of his sense of smell when it was the odours of dogs that were in question. The larger lesson that he learnt was that one should never get between a very hungry animal and his prey unless one is strong enough to fight the aggressor. Lastly he learned how and when ult animals co-operate to save every species from a common danger, but that though the killers and the victims co-operate with one another under terrible stress, they return to their old relationship as soon as the common danger is removed. Here men might be superior to beasts. They could help one another so that they need never go back to fighting, killing and war. Man can achieve what beasts do not.

13

spell of fear

'Compared with the emotion-odour of an animal, the other odours are quite negligible. And of all the emotion-odours the one that we can best recognize is that of fear. Fear marks its victims another way, also. A totally frightened animal either runs in a circle or cannot run at all. "Bahadur, my son, remember that well. Whenever you feel you are running in a circle more than twice, be sure you are afraid. And the only way to loosen the grip of fear from yourself is to stand still and think of being calm. This frees you; it always breaks the strings that bind you."

'I spoke in the above manner to my son, the day Ajit, the old elephant, now past a hundred, and I went on an excursion in the spring when Bahadur was on the threshold of his fourth year. It was a very unusual spring, coming very early and lingering long. The foothills of the Himalayas burst into colours, odours and sounds unheard of in a thousand years. Fragrance upon fragrance, bird-call upon bird-call, and colour upon colour spun and wove their choking abundance hour after hour. A little after sunset we were granted a respite from their myriad assaults upon our senses. The day-sounds were hushed by the waterfalls singing to the moon. The lilacs shook their fragrance upon our tusks and trunks. The moonlight put the colours to sleep. Clouds tip-toed from height to height on crystal feet, while the valleys and crags were filled with cchoes like humming birds,

'Now that Bahadur was older and stronger, he had to be instructed in the deeper things of life. I decided to tell him less of the facts and more about the emotions that animate them. And it was natural that I should teach him about fear, for it is the most universal thing in jungle-life. That spring-morning we three—Ajit first, Bahadur second and I last—set out for adventures. The monkeys from above shook many boughs and plucked many buds. Without eating it, they flung most of what they gathered below on the grass. There the barking deer were grazing by twos and threes, eating the gifts of the Hanumans. By their noises the monkeys informed their guests on the ground who was passing. But when we came along, instead of the tree-dwellers, the four-footed ones saw us. Since we had come upon them suddenly they were a bit frightened, so they set up barking "Khakkar, Khakkar," in a rasping manner which brought the monkeys down a few feet below. Now hanging by two hands to branches just above us, they examined our three backs. I snorted at them, which meant that all was well. Instantly they returned to their previous perch, cursing the deer as they went. Now these became quiet and continued to graze as before. For a while the jungle became still save for the hammering of the woodpecker on the trees.

'They and another creature make peculiar noises in the Spring. Woodpeckers hit the timber with their bills to get at some insects in all seasons but one. During the mating time they do not hammer into the log for their dinner. They are so deeply in love that they forget food and hunger, and hit oftener in the Spring than at any other time. These poor fellows have no voice with which to make a love-song, so to please their mates they hammer on the hardest wood or stone instead. Even at night if the moon shines brightly they hit their nests in their sleep, I am told. Be that as it may, is it not a strange way to make love? All this I explained to Bahadur, who had begun to observe everything.

'As we left the woodpecker behind, we reached a lake full of lotus buds. There we heard a noise that rose above all the others. It was not the bees. At this time of the year there is no lake without a lotus, no lotus that does not drench the air with its fragrance, and no fragrance that does not call the bees, and no bees that do not hum. But the sound that held our attention was like grass rubbing against a tiger's hide above us in the air. It was most uncanny. Slowly the sound came down and passed beneath us over the water. Who do you think made that noise? It was the snipe playing for his mate. The wind in brushing some of his tail feathers made the sinister-sounding song. It amused Bahadur greatly.

'Once his curiosity about the odd sounds had been satisfied, he began to notice the common spring noises. We heard the Kokil, cuckoo, singing and trying to decide in which bird's nest to deposit the eggs of the present season. The Bulbul, too, was singing when he was not too busy devouring insects.

'At that moment we heard a high shriek of "Khakkar, Khakkar, Khakkar," from a barking deer. It shocked Bahadur so that Ajit thought that we had better look into the trouble that the poor fellow was in. At first we expected to find nothing, for these deer are so peculiar that they sometimes bark without any cause, so we moved on without undue haste. But that did not last long, for in a few seconds a strong odour of fear struck our nostrils which made us hurry. We must find out the cause of that! Swiftly but silently we walked. The very grass on which we stepped stood up the moment we left it; so lightly were we treading! In the meantime the deer's cry grew heart-rending. Fortunately we did not have far to go. There in an open space stood a brown deer, his eyes fixed on a spot in the grass, his spine bent concave with terror, and his mouth emitting gruesome howls. Our elephant eyes are not very sharp. Instead of looking carefully at the grass we moved nearer to him. In spite of the growing intensity of the odour of fear, we hoped to find nothing dangerous before the Khakkar. Then, like a streak of black lightning, something moved almost at our feet. The shock of it made all three of us, young and old, stop and tremble, for we had beheld a large serpent with icy eyes looking at us. In an instant it had lunged forward swift as death. Fortunately, too late! Instead of coiling around its prey, the python fell by the deer. It had just missed!

'The python's spring coat flashed forth steely barbs of fire as it slid and glided in the sunlight to take one more aim and strike a second time at the flying deer. But the latter could not be killed by ten snakes now, for he had recovered from his spell of terror. In a trice he had bounded out of the enemy's reach.

'We too followed his example. For the stench of fear that his breathing and perspiring had left behind almost suffocated us. Besides, we did not like the looks of the angry serpent.

'After we had withdrawn to a safe spot I explained to Bahadur who was questioning me, why the reptile missed its kill. We had come upon both of them suddenly, and Bahadur, suspecting no trouble, had walked on almost between the killer and its victim. In order to protect him, Ajit and I pushed ahead, guarding the boy on the left and right. The serpent turned his eyes in our direction; and that very moment the Khakkar's eyes were freed from the hypnotic power that had held them. If the killer and its prey are interrupted in looking at each other, this is bound to happen. Slowly and laboriously the deer had lifted his head and gazed at us. As if this cut the chain that bound him to the spot, he moved a foot or so to his right. The python now feeling that his prey was beginning to regain his will-power, made the fateful lunge, and…missed. Was it not fortunate that we had come just in time to break the spell that his eyes had cast over the whole body of the deer?

'Now the question is, had we any right to interfere between an animal and its legitimate dinner! I informed Bahadur that had he not been with us we would not have gone out of our way. All old elephants are so used to noises that they are not curious enough to investigate them. Besides, we knew only too well that a snake who had had nothing to eat while he was hibernating all winter must satisfy his hunger. Therefore we would not turn aside to protect an animal from him. It is the business of the jungle gods and not of pachyderms to teach snakes vegetarianism. If the reptiles have not been elevated to the same state of refinement in eating vegetables as the elephants have attained, all that we can do is to help save those of the serpents' prey whom we stumble upon by chance. Beyond that we cannot go.

'No other adventure befell us that day. And seeing that we had had enough for the time being we decided to graze on the lake shore before returning to the herd. In order to make the lesson of the day clear to Bahadur I repeated: "Fear kills an animal long before its enemy pounces on it. Never be frightened, my son. Now you know definitely what the odour is. The barking deer naturally has no strong scent. But when it is frightened it exudes a terrible stench, nearly as bad as decaying meat! You can tell it from a great distance.'

14

bahadur tells his story

'Oh! my mother, since you command me, I shall relate what befell us—you, Ajit and myself. It was unexpected and overwhelming.

'You remember that the entire herd was moving against the clamorous wind and that we three were bringing up the rear. We could only vaguely hear the sounds made by those ahead of us, and no matter how loud the noise made by us, it could not be heard against the storm and by the elephants six feet ahead. As the wind rose to its uttermost fierceness you could get no other odour, and no sound save its sustained mounting shrieks. Boughs broke and fell so fast that they screened the herd before us from our view. My short legs made my strides small and slow, and mother and Ajit had to give up their usual swinging walk in order to protect me which made us fall yards behind the others. I cannot understand why the rest of you never looked back, Oh my father! Apparently you were pressing on so laboriously against the wind that you never knew when we had dropped completely out of your ken.

'As ill luck would have it, a mammoth plane-tree loaded with monkeys fell in front of us. In the confusion of falling monkeys and crashing trees we were held up many minutes. I was shaken out of my wits. Can you imagine a tree thick as an old elephant, tall as the stars, loaded with frightened jabbering Hanumans collapsing at your feet without your swerving from your path? We were not only shaken, but we lost our way.

'By the time we had recovered our senses and gotten our bearing the forest fire broke out. How did that happen? We supposed that a branch of the falling plane-tree rubbed and grazed a bamboo clump so that the friction that ensued set fire to the whole thing. Even if we do not know exactly the cause, there is no doubt that the bamboos burst into flames after the fall of the tree.

'We ran from the fire and of course our panic took us further away from the direction of the herd. Not only that, we had grown so panicky that we came right back to the fire after running about at top speed.

'But, mother is correcting me. You are right, my mother, the wind had spread the fence of flames in a vast arc. Just as we were at the height of terror, the other animals joined us. Tigers, stags, leopards, big buffaloes and wolves hung on to us hoping that we would lead them to safety. And lo! instead of that, we went round and round in a circle.

'That was it! The moment I had realized that fact it seemed to cut at least one link of the circle of fear! Now that I stood still, fear began to fall from my eyes as darkness vanishes in daytime by lifting our eyelids. I saw clearly what was the matter with all of us. Without delay I began to trumpet lustily for you, my father. I shouted for the Chief of our herd, for he alone could bring it to our rescue. How I did scream for you. I raised my tone higher and higher—each time I bellowed. Scream by scream, pitch by pitch, my voice climbed till it struck the right note: the note we use when we are in great trouble. It is the cry for the Chief.

'At last my voice cracked. I could trumpet no more. But by shouting so hard I had broken, totally broken, through the spell of terror. All of us now stood still. We waited and waited till we heard your thunder-call of succour, father. Though we were hemmed in by the fire—though the direction from which you called was screened with thick smoke, we had recovered from our fear sufficiently to come through it. The smoke choked and blinded us. But we obeyed our ears that had been hearing your call. The fire and smoke had no further terror for us.

'The stags, the tigers and the other animals followed our example. They, too, broke through the wall of smoke. Now all are safe, they and we.'

15

circle of fear

The circle of fear is as dangerous to elephants as it is to any other animal. A beast caught in it rarely makes good its escape. Though invisible it is more potent than the visible. Though intangible, it does more harm than a Kheddah trap, a hole in the ground, or a noose made of thongs. Moreover, an elephant can never be caught by any one of these others if he be not first caught in the trap of fear.

'I had to teach Bahadur all about this circle shortly after our meeting the python and the deer. One afternoon in the month of May when everything was crackling with the heat, we came upon a strange sight on the outskirts of the forest where there was a river. We had covered our backs thickly with leaves torn from trees above and from the grass on the ground. After having put on this sunshade, we could expose ourselves, without danger, to the sun. As we walked, if some leaves fell off our backs, we put on new ones to take their place.

'Protected in this manner we had travelled at least three miles when we reached the river, where we had our bath and swam about for fun. Before sundown we came out of the water and waited for the passing of the twilight. All the animals remained still as the Sun God sank into the night. Silence, cowled in black, walked into the jungle. After we had performed our adoration the jungle-priest, the bison, bellowed far off. The owls hooted, bats fanned the air with a soughing sound, and panthers mewed as they sprang down from the trees. Soon the voices of other animals joined in.

'Instead of going on we waited where we were for the moon to rise. This did not take long. Soon fell arrows of silver, setting the stream on fire. As the Deity of Night ascended the sky, the rabbits—at least a score—as if to do Him special homage, came out of their holes under the grass and danced in the moonlight. Some of them drummed the ground with their feet. Because they delighted in the radiance that fell from Heaven, they spread out in the open where there was more of it. It was marvellous for the young Bahadur to see the dance of the bunnies, his first sight of the magic effect upon them of moonlight. He squealed with pleasure. But hardly had the noise of it died down when he had to groan with surprise. For a menace of some evil thing beset the little dancers. They knew no more about it than we did, until the evil thing drew nearer. At last … the horror was upon the scene! I could tell by the smell who it was—Mr and Mrs Fox. They stood against the soft breeze and let it carry their scent to the dancing rabbits. It took them by utter surprise. They began to run about without thinking. The foxes, instead of running after them, moved only a few paces forward.

'This surprised Bahadur very much. For he had never before seen such tactics followed by any beast of prey. The two foxes simply waited in readiness to leap and kill. Bahadur was amused at this obvious silliness. He thought the bunnies had made good their escape, and that the still crouching killers were only funny. Just then a noise stung him. Behold! the little fellows were running back!

'"They are caught in the circle of fear," I muttered to my son. He did not understand me at first. I explained: "The rabbits are so frightened that they have lost their heads and are running right back into what they fled from. They are caught in the circle of fear." Hardly had I explained this when the foxes now leaped to the attack. It was so sudden that they killed two ere we could interfere. The little fellows were frightened anew by the sight of their dead friends and again ran away, while the foxes waited as before in the alert posture of attack. Then, alas, in a few minutes the terrified bunnies again returned to the same spot. The foxes were about to bound forward once more to kill. But at that moment a deafening noise struck them still. Bahadur roaring and raging charged at them like a storm unleashed.

'The noise that he had made was so great that it broke the circle that fear had flung round the rabbits, and they dashed away in straight lines in different directions. Seeing their prey escape them the foxes snarled.

'But now it was their turn to be frightened. Their snarl had brought Bahadur down on them like an avalanche. Had they been less nimble in dodging elephants' feet than usual, they would have been trampled into nothing. They escaped not a moment too soon from Bahadur's feet.

'That evening my son could not go to sleep. So we stayed up late and discussed the circle of fear. Whenever an animal is frightened he tends to run in a circle; it does not matter whether he is a man lost in the snows or an elephant who has lost his head. But, talking of fear makes some people feel fear, so after a while in order to change the subject I invited Bahadur to swim in the river. It was, I think, the first midnight swim of his life. He enjoyed it greatly and the next morning I heard him bragging about it, but I am glad to say that he did not mention his good work of saving the bunnies from the two foxes. It is a rule of the herd that good deeds when mentioned by him who does them, cease to be good.

'A month later another experience befell us which convinced Bahadur that the circle of fear is the door of death, and that one should never get caught in it.

'I have already mentioned that the month of May was very hot; moreover it did not rain at all. A miniature drought had set in. As the undergrowth of the jungle dried up, the suspicion of a big drought and of a forest fire dawned in our minds. No matter how far south and east we went, the Heavens shed not a drop of rain and rivers were no deeper than the width of a grass-blade.

'If two kinds of grass shrivel up in the heat, forest fires are imminent. Wherever the grass in the deep jungle turns brown, be sure the drought is complete, for there the sun usually cannot penetrate. The foliage between the sun and the ground is not only thick but almost impenetrable. When such a place is pierced by the Lord of Light and reduced to a state of utter dryness, what more evidence do you need of a real drought?

'But unless the second species of grass, the bamboo clumps, run dry, the chance of fire is no closer. The bamboos drive their roots longer into the earth, as you know, and when the wind blows, they rub against one another. It happens now and then that if they are dry and rub, the friction produces fire. Like a torch in the hand of a madman, the wind carries sparks from one burning clump and sets fire to the dry grass below.

'So Bahadur along with the rest of us had to be careful that summer. During the daytime if the herd was not travelling he, Ajit, his mother and I generally milled about together. Ajit taught him a lot of jungle secrets that had escaped my knowledge and scrutiny.

'A few weeks after his fourth birthday we were loafing in an immense forest of sal, tal, tamal and bamboos. The last named were so dry that they looked like torches ready for lighting. The wind was blowing on them furiously. Each stick rubbed hard against its neighbour though they grew inches apart. It looked dangerous. Ajit insisted that we had better clear out of this particular forest. The wind was increasing in fury every second. Pretty soon sal branches began to crash down on our backs, and uprooted trees fell almost in our faces. No one was frightened by this, but lest a falling tree hit and bury a young hathi under it, the herd decided to search for open country. So we started in single file.

'Hardly had we gone an hour when news came to me from the rear that Ajit, my wife and Bahadur had been cut off from us by falling trees, and we must wait till they rejoined us. So we waited. All about us, near and far off, we could discern above the surge and crash of falling trees, the gnashing and grinding of bamboos. It sounded like giants grinding their teeth in the dark.

We felt restive under such noise. Everyone's nerves began to get on edge. Still there was no news from my family and old Ajit. I refused to worry much because the wisdom of the ancient Ajit would extricate my son, no matter what scrape he got into. Though the herd squealed and clamoured for orders for marching on, I held fast to where we were.

'Far off we heard trumpeting in the rear, faint as a reed crying against a hurricane. It stopped. We waited with ears flung wide open. Even the minutest noise could not escape us now. In a minute more the same point of noise like a thorn pricked the hide of the hurricane.

'"Khan-na-phong," I shouted … "Rescue—To their rescue—Phong-na-Khan!" Hardly had I shouted twice when we ran down wind swifter than a python's strike. I was glad of our speed, particularly when I heard flocks of birds and monkeys screeching at one another above our heads, and the trumpeting far off was growing louder and louder.

'The monkeys were shouting "Fire, fire." So were the birds. But because it was downwind for a while we got no scent nor sight of it. Still we hurried on, everyone murmuring that both monkeys and birds couldn't be wrong. This spread panic in our midst, for no animal cares to go towards a forest fire. But I would not let them turn back. Without waiting to look whether they followed me or not, I hurled myself forward, swift as the leap of a leopard.

'There! Now there was no mistake…I got the scent of fire. And then what I saw thrust me close to the circle of fear! May the Gods of the elephants preserve me from seeing such a sight again! Lo! there were my wife, son, and Ajit leading a herd of buffaloes out of a ring of smoke. Bahadur first, Radha next, Ajit last. Presently they drew nearer, all three aching with burns. Slowly they came forth. After them a string of bisons who in turn led three panthers. Behind these cats, deer of all descriptions thronged. But instead of waiting to see each one of them emerge from the smoke-veiled jungle I went forward and put my trunk around Bahadur just to sustain him with my strength for he was fairly dropping with fatigue. Thus with my help he led the procession of beasts till all joined our herd who were most delighted to see us all alive. Two elephants put their trunks around the two tusks of Ajit to sustain him, and two others put their trunks around Bahadur which released me. Now I went to my wife's side. She, to my utter surprise, was the least burnt. She informed me that Ajit and Bahadur insisted on standing between her and the fire.

'But before she could tell me all about their misadventure, the clamour of monkeys from the trees and the stampede of beasts filled the jungle. "Lead, lead, lead," they were shouting. At that I put my trunk up and sniffed the air. Yes, there was no mistake about it. The fire was drawing nearer and nearer. "Ghawm, gon gon," I trumpeted. "Danger, silence," repeated the whole herd after me. "Ghawm, gon gon," rose like a thunderclap and silenced all the jabbering monkeys and the rest. In the ensuing stillness with the tip of my trunk I took observations. East, West, North—I sniffed the air in every direction. At last the compass of my nostrils told me of the exact direction of the fire. No sooner had I made sure of that than I gave the command to march. Slowly but fearlessly we moved. In perfect repose we trod away from the circle of fear.'

16

bahadur's initiation

Soon Bahadur's education was finished. After he had passed his seventh birthday, his little sister was born. She was about the same size and weight as himself when he came into this world.

With the arrival of the new offspring, his parents ceased to pay every attention to Bahadur. Moreover, now that he was big, Ajit and the rest made it clear to Radha and Sirdar that as soon as possible Bahadur should be treated not as their son but as any other member of the herd. Both his parents agreed to that and Ajit agreed to initiate the boy into his new status.

By initiation the animals mean the same thing as we do when we say that a boy or girl has come of age. The coming of age of his son made the task of Sirdar rather difficult. For it was not easy to treat one's son only as another elephant and no more. If the latter made any mistakes he had to be punished without mercy. If he went wrong, his father could do no better by him than he would have done for any other hathi of the herd.

Before going off on a few weeks' travel with Ajit for the purpose of his initiation, Bahadur was permitted to stay with the herd awhile. In exchange for that concession he was given some hard tasks to perform. Some of them proved most arduous and intricate. And to the joy of his parents he did his work well. But no doubt Radha and Sirdar kept their pleasure a secret!

Occasionally Bahadur was given the leadership of all the elephants of his age. He had to lead them in play as well as at work. If they had not enough to eat it was his duty to eat less than his share and give the rest to the others. If they got into trouble it was his business to face and overcome it.

Thus two months passed. At last, towards autumn, it was decided that Ajit should take Bahadur and go off on a few weeks' march ahead of the herd in order to teach the youth his final lessons in elephant-wisdom. So, without any show of grief at the thought of separation from his family, Bahadur trotted off with the venerable centurion.

This was in the autumn of 19— memorable for its partial drought in the south, and a dire flood in the north.

Owing to intense dry heat all of the month of July, miles of the southern forests turned into russet and orange many weeks before autumn. Since there was so very little water there, all the animals turned north where, they learned from wandering birds, monkeys and others, the green had not left the trees and grass, and the taste of fruits, leaves, and roots was more delicious than anywhere else.

Drawn by such good news, Ajit and Bahadur went to the pastures of Garwhal. Seen from this elevated plane the Himalayan peaks looked superb. Above the immediate verdant foothills the white summits, instead of flaming into red at sundown, were wrapped in violet, silver, purple and carmine. Every sunrise the ranges crouched at the threshold of Heaven like lions of amethyst.

There was something ominous in the hills below the snow line. Everything seemed too still to the aged Ajit. It was as if the gods were powerless to prevent an appalling danger sweeping down from heaven-haunting heights.

One fact anyone could grasp: the snows were melting fast, too fast. That is why water was abundant in the foothills and their vegetation intensely green. But the limited intelligence of the animals prevented them from seeing one obvious sign that lay at their feet: namely, the soil was damp, which was unnatural for the plateaus of Garwhal. Somewhere above, the swift melting of the snow was overflowing rivers and lakes and breaking through ridges. With soft snake-like movement it was breaking up a whole mountainside, then seeping its way down to the plains. This the beasts of the jungle could not calculate and discover when they crowded the lower Garwhal. It teemed with life. Every tree was bent low with the weight of monkeys and parakeets. Each river seemed to wear a necklace of kingfishers on its breast. Bellowing buffaloes, deep-throated Samburs, and roaring elephants thronged the place. This year each twig and every bush tasted more lush than at any time before. Rivers ran so high that they threatened to overlap their shores. If a stag or a buffalo bull, in order to drink copiously, got down into the water he never came out of it: the current swept him away like a leaf or a twig. Something sinister possessed the place, yet all the animals seemed to come to that valley driven by hunger and thirst.

Probing his memories of a hundred summers, Ajit told Bahadur that this kind of abundance in nature there foreboded certain calamity. They should get out of Garwhal soon. But they must wait for their herd, scarcely one week's march behind them if it had marched as arranged.

In the meantime the food and drink of the place tasted so sweet that strange new herds of elephants came there each day and packed the place. In order to avoid them, Ajit went off with Bahadur into the remoter parts. They went into the Country of the Nilgais, the cows who look green-blue, like the green forests. Whenever autumn strikes the Himalayan foothills, many animals come down to the warmer grounds below. So the ibet descend to the lower plateaus, and the nilgais with their green coats pasture further down in forests of tropical verdure, since their skins find protective colouring only in green forests. This particular year Ajit found them still in the upper plateaus which they had no notion of quitting, though the hour of doing so was at hand. Was it not autumn? Yet that incendiary of the seasons had not applied his red to a single tree! This was most unusual. The place was so green that it gave the nilgais protective colouring and also no end of good food. Why go farther south? Each animal was content to be where he was. The uncanny verdure lay like a trap. It proved too much for Ajit's wisdom—why was nature so generous this year? Young Bahadur paid no attention to the old fellow's questioning and probing. He enjoyed his dinners each day and his freedom without the herd, and played at chasing the growing nilgai steers.

It was during one afternoon's play hour that he felt a strange sensation. As he was putting his trunk around a young nilgai he became aware of hoof-beats accompanied by an awful bleating noise above from a high rock. So holding his trunk aloft he listened.

Thud, thud, thud-d-d and Baa-Baa-boom, came like a cataract. All the echoes shook with the noise.

Now the blue cows about him began to bellow with all their strength.

In order to find out from Ajit what this all meant, Bahadur ran down toward where that ancient was having his nap. But before be reached him a veritable stream of ibets began to pour onto the plateau. They rolled down from the Himalayas like fold upon fold of clouds. Seeing this descent upon themselves, the nilgais began to rush further below, vacating the plateau as fast as they could. But the ibets, instead of stopping there continued to rush further on, and Bahadur wedged himself between herds of blue cows and sheep in the direction of Ajit.

But he did not have to go far, for the old tusker was coming up to find him. As soon as he caught sight of Bahadur he signalled the youth to run faster than ever, for, as he explained to him, they were in the way of a vast sheet of water coming down from the high hills.

Now they hastened southwards almost in a straight line to bring news of the coming disaster to the herds of elephants. In order to do so they had to run along a river bank.

Alas, it was too late! Ere they had gone a mile, the river seemed to rise rapidly, sweeping them off their feet. Cataracts of water burst upon them from every direction. Soon they lost their footings. Now, turning and tossing in a swirling flood, they swam for their very lives.

All about them rushed drowned flocks of deer, nilgais and mountain sheep. What miracle carried the two elephants safely down they could not tell but they floated thus for at least half an hour, when, lo, the deluge arrested itself in a whirlpool formed against a man-made dam.

The two of them were bumped and bruised by floating trees in the ever-rising waters. Again and again they tried to fling their trunks around a tree standing on the shore in order to steady themselves. But as ill luck would have it, the water had loosened the roots so that a hathi's tug brought it down almost on his head. What were they to do before the dam broke, and they hurtled down a precipice to perish unlamented by their friends and family?

Then Bahadur did a clever thing. Putting his front legs on Ajit's rear, and thus raising himself, he threw his trunk around a bough of a tree whose roots the water had just begun to touch. The current pulling one way and his trunk on the branch pulling another, created a force that flung him very near the base of the tree. As Bahadur let go the tree to whose bough he had clung, it fell in front of them, momentarily arresting the rush of and swirl of the waters.

Then, miracle of miracles, the tree, some of its titanic roots still holding the fallen trunk and its mammoth boughs slowly obeying the force of the water, pushed the two floating elephants shoreward. Behold, already their feet had touched ground! Bahadur, being young and light, climbed to shore without much difficulty. Now, he being the son of his father, instead of running to safety, stood where he was and stretched out his trunk, attaching it to Ajit's. Imagine an elephant two tons in weight pulling another weighing four tons and a half up an incline! Even at the risk of his own life Sirdar's son was going to save the ancient warrior from death. Despite the latter's slipping again and again, Bahadur held on. Thanks to the gods of the hathis for that—for had he not done so Ajit would have perished... Because of his hold, at last, after slipping the twentieth time, the latter's feet stood firmly on the ground. Lo, he was saved! Bravo, Bahadur! Just think of it—like a boy pulling a whale ashore—Bahadur drew Ajit into safety. And none too soon, for then the flood rose to its highest, and like the grinding of many thunders, burst the dam. A howling wilderness of water rushed past them. But they were safe.

Ajit and Bahadur were determined to find their herd and bring to it the news of the deluge. Of course the herd itself had been informed of the disaster by the real runners of the jungle—the birds and the monkeys. The former flew fast as the lightning and the latter, running from forest to forest like stallions that have broken their reins, spread the news of the calamity to all Garwhal and half of the United Provinces of Agra and Oudh.

Sirdar's herd, which had reached their appointed place where they were to meet Ajit and Bahadur, waited for the two as long as they could. Then hearing the 'surge and thunder' of the flood not far off, they formed their line with the Chief at the head and flew southeast, fleet as stags. But the flood overtook them. Had they not waited for Ajit and Bahadur they would have all made good their escape, but now they had to pay a heavy toll, less in numbers than in person bereavement, for Radha and her little daughter were among the drowned and the missing. She tarried too long for her son and did not mind lingering a few hundred feet behind the others in the fond hope of seeing him running towards her all safe and sound. Sirdar, who was far ahead, bent on leading the whole tribe out of the danger-zone, knew nothing of his wife's straggling behind. At the moment, he was doing his duty as the Chief—which excluded all special attention to his wife and daughter. Of such noble discipline is a true leader made. And had it not been for this self-sacrificing leader, the herd would never have made good its escape at such a small cost as the lives of a dozen of its members.

Sirdar had taken a southeasterly course and run out of the way of the deluge almost in time. Only the wilful loiterers who straggled too far in the rear out of the reach of his eyes, ears, and trunk were drowned. Radha, he learnt later, had actually died in an effort to save a life.

Now on a plateau of safety against a high hill to the east, the herd took shelter. Here like a bolt from the blue the news of the death of his wife and child smote the Chief.

But to him the blow was still heavier for he assumed that Bahadur too had been lost. For an instant woe laid siege upon him like triple torture. Unable to believe that his wife was dead he ran about looking for her like one mad. He dashed through herds of goats, nilgais, elephants, buffaloes, and others, looking for his family. Though the animals told him that they had seen them swept into the flood, he refused to believe their word. Sorrow had so bereft him of his senses that he did not trumpet either to ease his heart or to call his nearest and dearest ones.

Poor Sirdar—what a price he had to pay for being a leader. He could not succour, nay, was not permitted even to look back at his own wife and child when they needed him most. What a horror a leader's life must be! He must live and die for others and not for his own family.

It has been already mentioned that had he not forgotten to trumpet he would have found at least some solace, for in that crowd of thousands of beasts was Bahadur who though unseen was able to hear his father's voice. Had Sirdar only trumpeted as he ran hither and yon....

Ajit and Bahadur, who were standing on the same

plateau of safety where the living members of their herd had taken refuge, now learned from the other creatures what it was that unloosed such a deluge upon the world. Out of many strange tales the following fact emerged. A ridge of the Himalayas that had been slowly cracking for months had broken and emptied an immense mountain lake into Garwhal, which not only overflooded old waterways but sent the flood in new streams, and swept villages and forests out of existence. It killed ten thousand human beings, untold deer, tigers, hathis, leopards, buffaloes, monkeys, snakes and other animals.

On their way to the plateau of safety Ajit and Bahadur came across all kinds of frightened beasts running in circles. They found them in strange combinations: for example, monkeys waltzing helter skelter all over the woods with leopards, and here and there stags and tigers skipping about like fellow vegetarians frightened out of their wits, and pythons lying coiled at the feet of barking deer.

Compared with these frightened creatures, the two elephants were the very backbone of courage. Just to prevent themselves from being carried away by the fright of others, the old elephant and Bahadur decided to lead the terrified beasts out of their present trouble. Ajit being dead tired Bahadur took the matter into his own hands. His short, sharp calls fell like a sledgehammer on the consciousness of the fear-bound animals. The cries set them free. All of them stopped running around like lunatics. Though they had ceased to fear, they were too dazed to do anything of their own initiative. In order to keep them from relapsing again, Ajit too trumpeted with all his might. Then with his tusks he prodded Bahadur from behind, meaning 'Lead,' which made the youth start at once. The others followed meekly, only too glad to get out of that region of terror and death. Thus led by a child, they had reached the same plateau of safety where the young leader's father had brought his followers and was looking everywhere for his two children and Radha.*

* At this writing, the late summer of 1928, a similar emptying of a mountain lake is expected in the Himalayas.

17

bahadur comes of age

It had not been easy to lead a tired elephant more than a hundred years old and a large variety of wild beasts dazed with terror. But Bahadur did it well. He went without food, drink, and sleep for hours.

It had been easy to lead the crowd on to the plateau of safety while daylight lasted. Now, after nightfall, new difficulties presented themselves. One of these proved hard enough to destroy all hope. About ten o'clock at night Bahadur found that the droves of animals who had poured onto the plateau of safety had overcrowded it. They must move further on if they were to find pasture and hunting ground for all.

But alas, there was no place to move into. To the east rose the mountains like a knife, up which only a few goats could climb. To the south about half a mile away, stretched a flooded valley. Whether the water was deep or shallow none could tell. The thousands of animals could make out no more by the noise of the waters than that a rapid current was running, the very sound of which frightened them so that they stood still where they were. None had the courage to step in and fathom its depth. Fear and wonder had wrought havoc in their hearts and not one in those innumerable flocks had a shred of initiative left. Like a beaten army they were waiting to be wiped out by the enemy.

Every hour the fear in the minds of the others communicated itself to those of the few newcomers who kept straggling in. Perceiving the spread of this contagion, Bahadur and Ajit decided to ford the flooded valley. 'Better perish in an effort to cross than die of fearing,' was their motto. Ajit, who was eleven feet tall, stepped into the stream. Lo, it went just above his ankles and no more. Exhilarated by that happy surprise, he trumpeted to broadcast the good news. Bahadur, who had followed his example, shouted 'Khonta, ta ta ta! Khonta, ta ta ta—Come, even I am fording it.' He repeated this cry many times.

Only elephants understood him but in five minutes one large elephant loomed behind him. He said 'Tonha, tono—lead, my son, I follow you.' It was Sirdar!

Father and son put their trunks around each other. Sirdar's heart nearly broke with the sense of comfort at finding at least one member of his family alive.

But his joy was not allowed any further expression at the moment. For Ajit was trumpeting 'Ghoom, grunt ghoom—This is no time for rejoicing. Follow me closely.'

'Bonk,' grunted back Sirdar, meaning: 'I obey your orders.'

Here it may be pointed out that a true leader knows how to follow implicitly a superior when occasion demands. That Ajit's years of experience made him the superior, for the present crisis, there is no doubt. So when he ordered, not only Bahadur, but Sirdar too obeyed meekly.

As they walked ahead they found that the water was not too high anywhere. It rarely came up to Bahadur's chest, which fact made them walk less gingerly than before. Even so it seemed as if it would take many hours to reach the opposite shore: the flood appeared to have spread itself on a fabulously wide, flat country. This was fortunate, for if the stretch of land not been flat and far-flung the current that the elephants were traversing would have been deeper and more fierce.

Seeing them go ahead other members of their herd followed. Then after them came the unknown herds.

About two-thirds of the way across they reached a deep hole where the water swirled menacingly by. After hesitating a while in front of it, Ajit stepped forward. The water came up instantly, almost touching his hips. This Bahadur observed from behind the centurion. But seeing his leader go on and out of that hole Bahadur stepped forward like a soldier marching to his death.

In an instant, leaping forth like a lion, Sirdar came up abreast of his son. It was fortunate that he did so for the water had risen high as the youth's throat and its force was carrying him away. Like a vast liner against a small boat he stood guard over the only surviving member of his family. Though the current buffeted and beat at the boy it could not sweep him off because his father stood firm as a mountain.

Looking behind, Ajit saw Bahadur's predicament and quickly walked backwards standing on the other side of him between the current and the youngster. His body acted like a rock, slowing down the speed of the water. That very moment Bahadur found his footing and climbed out of the malignant depth. But from now on instead of walking before and behind him the two large hathis walked alongside of him in order to protect his flanks. Fortunately they came across no other danger-spot during the rest of their journey through the watery waste.

But that sinister deep hole produced a bad effect on the hathis that had been following them. Their nerve had been so shaken by the sight of Bahadur's latest struggle against drowning that they refused to move. Moreover, they did not have courage enough to try another tack, so there they stood petrified for hours.

It was past midnight when our three adventurers reached the opposite shore, where the earth was solid and the jungle endless. What a glorious moment! Now they arranged that one of them should go back to the frightened animals on the edge of the deep hole. Naturally Sirdar volunteered.

But ere he had gone a dozen paces when with a ghastly groan of pain, Ajit fell on his four knees and buried his tusks deep into the ground. Sirdar turned and ran back quickly to his friend's side. Bahadur was already near him. Now father and son put forth their trunks and worked hard to raise Ajit to his feet. It took a great deal of labour to do so for the heart attack that he had had was serious. The Chief and his son sustained him with their strength awhile after the attack had passed. Even half an hour later, Ajit proved too feeble to stand all by himself. So Sirdar put his trunk under his tusks anew, thus aiding him to keep his balance.

Finding the problem at hand difficult if not insoluble, Bahadur volunteered to recross part of the flooded area to those elephants who were still standing on the edge of the deep hole, in order to inform them that the crossing could be safely made. This was his duty. His father must agree, or give up supporting the stricken Ajit and go himself. A leader ought to do his duty. Bahadur had not strength enough to sustain Ajit on his feet; he must go and Sirdar remain behind.

This decision was made in a flash. There was no wordy dispute about it. Truth to tell, the returning alive of the young fellow would be the best proof to the frightened herds that there was nothing to fear. Though the father's mind was filled with the agony of doleful forebodings, in order to bring across to safety his own herd and others he had to consent to his son's venturing forth into the deluge.

Bahadur found the recrossing no easy task. You must remember that a current of water wears no footprint nor remains polluted with the odour of the beast that has crossed it. Unlike the earth and trees of the jungle a river retains no mark of those that traverse it. Bahadur, who had been brought up in the ways of the jungle all his life, found his solitary travel across the rapids most difficult, without odour, or mark of any kind to guide him. The flood had washed away all traces of himself, Sirdar and Ajit, long ago. In fact he had to make a new track in a virgin and hostile wilderness of flowing current. For every minute that he walked he watched and tested the water in front of him double that time before moving forward again. He concentrated his mind and will, determined to bring the good news to the frightened fellows yonder. So, no matter how laboriously, step by step, he went on and on.

Fortunately he did not have far to go. About three in the morning, long before he reached the deep hole, he heard the water splashing. This startled and stopped him. Again he heard splash, rush, splash! He said to himself: 'Who can this be? Is it the flood rising higher and gurgling more furiously? What must I do then?'

He shut his eyes and listened very carefully. While thinking and listening intently, the sounds of feet cutting through the current drew so close that they frightened him. Instantly he opened his eyes. A large tusker who had but one tusk was leading towards him an endless number of animals. Bahadur was elated with pleasure, and trumpeted to all the elephants, both of his own herd and those of others. Like a panther leaping on a stag, the mammoth came swiftly to his side. It was Kumar, his father's old rival and friend. Following him came numberless hathis. Kumar grunted at Bahadur, meaning 'Lead!' Bahadur turned and did as he was bid. Kumar followed close on his heels, and behind him a throng of trumpeting hathis and bellowing buffaloes.

All the noises beat upon the echo-laden spaces, making them howl like thunder gone mad. Buffaloes and samburs came through the water alongside of the hathis, and protected on one side by that rock-like mass, they too forded the flood. Thus almost a whole kingdom of animals, led by the youthful Bahadur, reached the other shore just as day was breaking. The spectacle that the sun beheld on his rising had never before been seen by him. Imagine to yourself two rows of animals held in maritime discipline, crossing a waste of rushing water! Here and there were elephants who did not complain if monkey mothers with babies rode on their backs. Such a vision of mutual aid pleased the Sun God that morning.

Bahadur, as soon as he put his feet again on the firm ground, trumpeted lustily. 'Earth, hard earth,' trumpeted after him all his followers.

As soon as they came out each kind of animal formed its own group or waited along the stream for other members thereof. Sirdar, to answer the trumpeting of his son, turned towards the river to greet him and the other members of his herd. At first he saw only Bahadur who, having just climbed up the bank, shut the elephant coming right after him from the Chief's view. The gladness of finding his return from his grave venture made Sirdar forget everything. For several minutes his happy eyes saw nothing but the heroic youth.

At last the odour of something aroused him from his happy mood. Following the direction of the odour his eyes caught sight of a strange shape. What was that? About half a dozen feet from him stood Kumar. A shudder ran through his own body. Elephants have the most tenacious memories. Both the old bachelor and the Chief had not only recognized each other but grown feverish with the shock of their sudden meeting. Sirdar was robbed of all initiative; nor did Kumar know what to do. Was he to move forward or turn right about and march off into the jungle?

'Yes, I had better go off,' he said to himself.

But as he turned and started on his journey he heard a groan of pain from an old elephant. The sound of the voice was so familiar that it drew him as much by its own quality as did the sight of the aged Ajit, again seized by a heart attack. Kumar reached his side from the left quicker than Sirdar did from the right. Now the two of them saved the ancient hathi from falling down again.

Seeing his father and the stranger engaged in their common act of mercy, Bahadur marshalled all the members of their herd together. It was then that the absence of his mother smote him painfully. She was to be found no more amongst them. What a dismal world he was doomed to live in!

'Dhon dhon dhon,' grunted his father at him. That meant 'Lead the herd into the jungle, boy, for pasture. We follow with Ajit.'

His duties pressed upon him so that Bahadur had no time to think of his personal pain. Such is the grim life of a true leader. He must neither be depressed by sorrow, nor elated by joy.

True to the ancient tradition of leadership, that young hathi swallowed his own feelings and set out to lead the herd in his father's place. Lo, at its end Kumar and Sirdar with friendliest cordiality assisted the stricken Ajit to follow the others. Were it not for the ancient elephant's strange illness the two friends would never have come together as they did.

18

mahaprasthan

After they had reached the heart of the forest Sirdar called the roll of his followers. It revealed a loss of eleven members of his herd, including his wife and daughter. But since public mourning is forbidden amongst wild animals the bereaved hid their grief from the rest of their tribe. Not only that—they were obliged to join in the rejoicing caused by their happy escape from death.

Since Bahadur was the centre of a good deal of attention it brought them a sense of consolation. Besides now they learnt from the other members of the tribe that Radha had died in the effort to save her little daughter who had fallen into the risen stream. This not only discredited the previous story that she had loitered far behind the herd for Bahadur but it established the noble fact that mother-love raises animals to the same height of self-sacrifice as human mothers.

In the meantime Bahadur was worried about his old teacher Ajit. That fellow had already relinquished his place of honour in the herd to Kumar, the stranger with one tusk. He kept close to the youngsters and the others all the time, moving about slowly with them and telling them all that he knew of life and nature. There was something distinctly sad and solemn in the air. Apart from gratitude to the great ancient the youth felt something strange impending. It is curious that the coming of death should make itself felt to the young. At least a week before Ajit died all the youngsters, including Bahadur, knew what was ahead.

Both father and son knew that the ancient warrior was dying of the effects of his strenuous work during the flood. He had caught a sinister cold and his heart had behaved in a wayward fashion ever since. Vigour was leaving his body as rapidly as the stars flee from the coming sun.

What a relief it would be to be saved at last from the bother of worrying about sickness and death. It is a well-known phenomenon that all wild animals meet death like a friend. They never resent its coming. Whatever is born must die. But the soul of a creature never dies because it is not born. The soul is never troubled by the birth and death of the body in which it lives.

Suddenly one day Ajit told the chief of his approaching Mahaprasthan—grand adventure. Now the time had come at whose end he must face the Sun of Immortality. Each yard that he covered, every blade of grass that he stepped on whispered 'Mahaprasthan—the grand journey.' 'This is the end,' he seemed to say to himself. 'I shall enter the House whence I came.'

Without any ado, after the midday meal when the members of the herd were taking their accustomed rest, Sirdar and Bahadur were invited to a walk with Ajit.

Soon they reached a lonely spot. It was dark and thickly covered with foliage. Even the all-seeing eyes of vultures and buzzards could not penetrate there. No sun shines there, nor falls the footfall of a star! This was the death-zone of elephants. Only he who is ready to die a natural death enters here. Without making a gesture, without looking back, Ajit the unvanquished entered the mansions of Silence…

On their way back to the herd Sirdar informed his son that unless an elephant is bitten by a snake or struck down by some other accident he prefers to go to death in the secret places of the forest, where no sun ever peeps, nor falls the silver spears of the moon.

In that august and inviolate realm an elephant embraces his brother, Death, and thus finds peace in the House of Perfection.

Oh, my Son, we can imagine Sirdar exclaiming further; 'You who will be the Chief of the Herd some day, do not grieve for the dead. But rejoice in the thought that he died at a great age finishing what he was born to accomplish. Now that he is happy in the company of the gods, rejoice you too on earth.'

19

how kumar met the herd

Long after his initiation was over, when Spring came again, Bahadur descended with the herd into the valley of the Ganges.

It has been already mentioned that Kumar was given the place of old Ajit in the tribe at the latter's request. He took a great fancy to all the young people, especially he liked Bahadur,

But before we go any further we must explain how he came to the flooded area and why he forded the stream at the head of the elephants.

The fact is that even that rogue had heard of the wonderful pastures below the Garwhal Hills. Thither went the lonely wanderer to satisfy his greed as did the others. The moment the lake broke through the high ridge and poured itself into the lower regions he ran for his life. Being alone he made good his escape into the plateau of safety. There the appalling number of animals crowded upon him so that his bachelor's mind, accustomed to solitude, grew excited.

Just then he beheld three elephants crossing the flood. This fired his imagination. When he saw some more elephants follow their example he too stepped into the water, and when, after what seemed hours of wading, the others in front of him stood still, he left his place and walked alongside the chain of elephants and reached the spot where they had been brought to a standstill. There he learned of the deep hole full of water that might drown them all. They were so shaken by their previous misadventures that they expected to die any moment. As Kumar was not frightened nearly as much as the others he went into the hole and came out of it without any difficulty, which put heart into the waiting chain of elephants. Then they swung along after him, and about a hundred yards from the shore he encountered Bahadur, who led them to the bank.

Since the rest of Kumar's story has been told already we shall recount now the adventure that befell the herd the spring of Bahadur's eighth year.

20

the final test

Kumar during the years of his solitary existence as a rogue elephant had developed some dangerous habits, for one of which the Chief of the herd had to pay almost with his life. It proved to be the severest ordeal for his character.

It is a well known fact that though the laws of India protect flocks of well-behaved hathis from the hunters, they provide not a very large margin of mercy for the ill-behaved, solitary rogues. A rogue is declared an outlaw the moment he harms a villager or his property. And since an outlaw can be shot for his ivory all kinds of rapacious hunters swoop down on him like vultures on a battlefield. Since to be human is to err, no hunter is punished by the law if in his effort to get at an outlawed rogue he kills a well-behaved hathi or two. Alas, since man makes his laws he favours man. Lo, often have we witnessed the killing of a good tusker because by accident he found himself between an outlaw and the hunter's rifle! Let us be thankful for one fact in nature, namely, that she makes only a few rogue elephants, otherwise, despite the human laws, the visiting foreigners and the hunters would have shot all the Indian elephants out of existence under the pretext of lulling the numerous declared outlaws. Indeed the hathis ought to thank their gods for the small number of rogues in the jungle!

The trouble that Sirdar and his herd fell into because of Kumar proved to be the effect of a chain of causes. We should follow them in their proper order.

After the autumn flood and the death of Ajit, the herd went south. And on their way Kumar acted according to the bad habits that he had formed during his rogue's days—one of which was his habit of preying on grain-fields. That year, owing to the catastrophes of nature, the wheat fields had suffered most. People valued wheat as if it were gold. Every field that grew it was considered sacred. No trespassing of any sort was permitted there.

But Kumar, who had grown to love stolen wheat for his supper, slunk out of the jungle at night and devastated meadows full of it during the herd's journey south. Seeing him doing it repeatedly other members of the flock began to follow his example. In two weeks' time Sirdar noticed that Kumar had half-ruined the usual sense of discipline among his followers. Every now and then some of the herd would steal out of sight and plunder grain-fields.

If all of them had had Kumar's knowledge of human nature it would have been safer, for the rascal knew full well where the watch kept by men on their wheat would be poor. Thither he would go and eat his fill and then make good his escape hours before detection. In short, Kumar was a professional, but those who followed him were amateurs. They soon fell upon fields that were well watched. In a few days more the entire countryside knew that a whole herd of elephants had gone lawless. They applied for the government's permit to send out licensed hunters to shoot the lot. But the latter, instead of granting this permission, detailed Ghond the famous hunter to observe the herd in order to determine its real character.

No doubt Ghond was a lover of animals. If he erred he would not do so in favour of man. When, after leaving the railway station, he penetrated the jungle of Gangapore, he learned from the peasantry whose fields had been visited recently by some of Sirdar's followers, that the leader of the outlaws was a hathi with one tusk. They christened him Eka Danta—One Tooth.

That night soon after moonrise Ghond the hunter sat on a tree on the border of the field and watched the going and coming of the animals. At first the leopards went into the fields and disappeared in the tall grain. Next came a tigress and her two cubs. They too vanished under the silver oblivion of moonlight that transfigured the wheat.

In another hour all the noise of the jungle meadows spun themselves into threads of magic. No one sitting on Ghond's tree would or could have bothered about watching anything. He would have let himself dream out the entire tropic night. But Ghond was no ordinary mortal. Resisting the witchery of sound and sight he crouched on his seat like a panther for its prey.

Suddenly a clamour of dry leaves like cackling birds smote his ear. He looked intently but could see nothing. Again the leaves cawed and crackled. Much nearer this time. And ere he had turned his head in the direction of the noise the tree on which he sat trembled as if tons were leaning against it for support. To a jungle-man like Ghond the thing was easily explained: a wild elephant had walked straight to his tree, and was now rubbing his side against it. The shadows striped his side and between the folds of his hide streaks of moonlight zigzagged like lightning.

After his first cursory look Ghond noticed that the beast under him had one tusk—'Ha, Eka Danta,' he exclaimed to himself. As if he had spoken out loud the tusker in question held his ears wide open in order to hear better. In that position he held them until some other elephants came and joined him. Then leading them he walked into the grain-fields. Ghond counted their number. They were eleven, all young males. Seeing them lift up the wheat by the trunkfuls he did his duty. He fired a blank shot from his rifle. This scared the crowd. All of them ran away, save one. Eka Danta remained. He stood still for a while; then hearing no further noise, busied himself with the wheat.

At last in order to stop him from wreaking havoc on the field Ghond came down from his perch and stood under the tree. The wind was from the tusker toward himself. But from him it blew into the jungle. That became quite clear to him; for in several minutes the ten hathis who had run away, now trumpeted loudly, giving the danger signal 'Ganga'—meaning 'Man.' Kumar, or Eka Danta, stopped eating wheat and dashed into the forest. He passed within a dozen feet of Ghond.

If Ghond thought he could breathe comfortably now he was mistaken. By putting his ear to the ground he could tell that the hathis were withdrawing, yet there hung in the air a feeling that something was impending.

Before he had lifted his head from the earth and stood erect he smelt cat. He raised his rifle in the direction of the odour. Now his eyes told him who was there. About a score of cubits from where he stood three pairs of emeralds were growing bigger and drawing nearer. Since his purpose was not to kill anything but to detect an outlaw flock he resisted all temptations to hunt cats. The tigress and her cubs were too near for him to attempt climbing the tree, and he put his back against it and waited. The emeralds instead of growing any bigger remained stationary. It seemed as if he must pass the whole night in this way: one man against three cats.

But the gods of the jungle had other things in view. On his left, not far away a large shape was appearing. But since only a quick glance and no more could be given to it Ghond did not quite know what it really was—a buffalo or a hathi. His eyes focused anew on the tigers. But they, in that instant were no longer there or, at least, their eyes had vanished. No doubt they had turned them toward the enormous shape coming down on them. The great hunter looked once more. What he now saw made his heart jump with pleasure and surprise. A mighty elephant stood there, his two tusks gleaming like upturned scimitars, his majestic brow hallowed with iridescence, his trunk a silver stream and his ears half open like giant fans. What a sight! The repose of that mammoth was so great that it reduced the tigers into three gaping children and himself into an awe-struck infant. Ghond said to himself: 'This must be the Chief of the herd come to examine the antics of his followers.' It was indeed Sirdar.

He had come to learn the kind of trouble Kumar had been storing up for himself and those two young hathis that went with him. The moment he saw Ghond with his gun the Chief surmised the whole situation.

It was fortunate for the old hunter that the leader of the hathis had appeared. For he first diverted, then caused the three tigers to run away. But instead of advancing on Ghond, like an apparition he vanished into the forest. Instantly the hunter, slinging his rifle on his shoulder by its strap, ran up the tree with the speed of a chipmunk.

The next day he informed the village that the whole flock was not bad, but there was no doubt that Eka Danta was an outlaw who needed punishing. Of course the villagers would not agree with him. They insisted that the whole flock should be put out of the way.

'Did you not see eleven hathis come down on us, O cousin of the owls?'

No matter what names they called him the old hunter would not agree to declare eleven hathis fit for shooting. He took good care not to mention that he had seen another, the twelfth, the most majestic tusker in India. For he feared lest their love of ivory would sway the people to declare the elephant an outlaw. After a great deal of wrangling the villagers and Ghond agreed on a proposal which they wired to the government at Calcutta. It read: 'One-toothed rogue should be declared outlaw stop in getting him six more elephants may be shot since he has very bad companions.'

You can see from the above that Ghond had succeeded in keeping almost half the number of undisciplined elephants from the vindictive village.

Now began the terrible part of his job. He was ordered by the government to lead seventeen English hunters, most of them tourists, to the Gungapore jungles in order to dispatch Kumar, at least.

Soon after the telegram was sent, the herd moved further to the southeast. It had followed and passed the Subarnarekha river to Mahapal. All this time Ghond too had to travel after it with his seventeen Englishmen on the tame elephants. The English hunters were Ledly, Carpenter, Bilton and Ellis. The last named was a captain in the British army while his two companions were civilians or members of the ICS (Indian Civil Service). It was easy for the humans to pursue the hathis for the latter had done damage to grain-fields wherever the jungle bordered on them, and like careless thieves had left clues behind. Ghond, who knew the country well, took his followers through a short cut to Mahapal several days before the herd had arrived there.

During this interval the state of discipline had reached such a low level that the hathis were virtually split into two herds: one of which did whatever Kumar proposed and the other half obeyed Sirdar implicitly. As luck would have it Kumar and his crowd were so bent on tasting every bit of wheat that lay by their way that they were delayed, and it was the Chief and his loyal band who reached Mahapal first.

There Sirdar's invincible sagacity told him at once that the jungle of Mahapal was humming with the hornets of death. For what are bullets but hornets that sting a hathi to death? Every kilometre that he trod gave out an odour of man. And so well hidden was the latter that nowhere could the herd locate him. An atmosphere of danger is more demoralising than its cause. So the constant presence of man in the jungle unnerved them all. Instead of going forward they hung back marking time. Even flank movements were impossible, for no matter how far they went to the right or left Ghond's scouts stood in their way.

After they had spent two days marking time the gay band under the careless Kumar came towards them. Instead of stopping to inquire the reason of their predecessors' halt, the whole flock walked right into the trap that Ghond and his hunters had laid for them.

Long before they were aware of the presence of men their rear had been closed by a hive of scouts and a tame elephant which carried a mahout, Captain Ellis and Ghond. Ghond ostensibly chose this position for himself so that he could drive forward the criminal band about three kilometres to a jungle at whose end was a vast clearing guarded by Carpenter and Ellis and thirteen other hunters on their elephants. No doubt all the Englishmen were determined to kill only Kumar the declared outlaw and none else, but man proposes and nature disposes, as we shall see.

As the wall of humanity pressed on after them, Kumar and his followers dashed ahead in order to escape it which was not a strategic thing to do, for they were in open country where stood a line of tame hathis. Ghond, who was a very wise jungleman since he had no enmity but only admiration for good herds like the one under Sirdar, left no guards nor orders to keep the tame elephants from moving wherever they pleased.

Thus it fell out that no sooner had the odour of man receded than the Chief led his followers in single file. But he took good care to have Bahadur walk next to himself. This was unusual but the herd obeyed their commander, since their faith in his judgment was absolute. Foot by foot with extreme caution they went after the receding phalanx of men at whose centre was one tame elephant. As if the whole jungle knew what was impending it grew clamorous with danger signals. Monkeys shrieked and shouted at the parrots, the parrots screeched with all their might, leopards and panthers unable to sleep in that din growled with anger while on the ground deer-folks scampered off in different directions, while wild buffaloes bellowed in anger. Of course this struck terror into the hearts of the scouts. Without much delay they left the floor of the jungle and took shelter within the trees, where the frightened monkeys spat out half-chewed nuts on their heads. It was most unpleasant but safer than being on the ground, so reasoned those frightened men.

Just then rifles barked in the not remote distance. A sinister silence followed. Then like a hundred raging rapids leaping from a riven rock the elephants under Kumar trumpeted in a heart-breaking manner—'Konk Konk Konk—retreat, retreat, retreat!' Again the rifles barked—phut, phut, phut! But that was drowned by the help call of Kumar and his friends 'Doom Konka, Doom Konka—help, Chief, help, help, help.' That cry of Kumar's struck the Chief's ear as if his own son had been hit by a bullet and was calling for succour in mortal agony. 'Honk,' he growled at his associates, meaning: 'Follow carefully.' Then with Bahadur he rushed to the rescue of his friends. Like a python he flashed and passed.

In a few minutes he drew within charging distance of the tame elephant that carried Ghond. Ere he could hit that beast from the rear the hunter had warned Captain Ellis, who had raised his rifle and fired. The Chief lowered his head to receive it, but instead of hitting his skull the bullet lodged itself in his shoulder. Now doubling the momentum of his attack in spite of the searing pain in his leg he flung himself on the tame tusker, and the fellow in utter panic fled out of sight, towards the open, not more than three hundred feet away. Had the Englishman, Ghond, and the Mahout not lain low and hung fast to the mattress on his back they would have been knocked off by the branches of trees under which they passed.

The flight of that elephant cleared the way, making safe the retreat for Kumar and his followers who rushed back into the jungle away from the bullet-ridden clearing where seventeen hunters were advancing on their mounts, and firing as they went.

In the dusk of the jungle Kumar and his friends saw dimly a pathetic sight. The Chief lay crouched on the ground in a pool of blood groaning with pain, while his son Bahadur was making frantic efforts with his small trunk to lift the master.

Kumar's heart was wrung with remorse. He went to Sirdar's other side and put his own one tusk and trunk under his two. Thus aided by Kumar on one side and by Bahadur on the other, Sirdar raised himself on his feet. Now that the shock of the bullet and the effort of the attack on the tame hathi had passed Sirdar found that he was not fatally wounded. He could stand on his own feet, at any rate, and order his friends out of danger.

Then, despite numerous trees in front of him, he perceived that many tame men-carrying-hathis were coming to attack the herd anew. 'Gre gromm—Attack, attack,' he thundered. Now began the fun of it. All the wild ones cleared their tusks, and stood a solid phalanx ready to do or die. The Chief thundered anew—'Attack, attack, no retreat, no retreat—attack!'

As if his inability to lead them had lent greater power to his commands the herd rushed to the attack. Heads down, trunks in their mouths, their ears stiff like sails taut in the wind, and their tusks ready to pierce oak or steel—they charged. 'Hum burra, Hum hurra,' they trumpeted in unison, crashing on breaking trees, trampling on panthers and wolves that got in their way, and with the fiercest fury they fell upon the man-bearing hathis.

Though more than one comrade dropped dead in his tracks yet they dashed on. The latter, despite all the shouts of their mahouts who jabbed their necks deeply with sharp ankuses fled like dogs before this tiger. All the jabbing ankuses in the world could not take them near the sharp tusks of the untamed ones. They dared not turn around and face the charge of their free-born wild cousins.

While unable to move, Sirdar, standing in one spot, conducted the operations of his flock. His strategy worked like a well-oiled machine. He trumpeted, groaned, and trumpeted again to give different kinds of orders. The herd having regained its sense of discipline, now obeyed him wholeheartedly. Thus they were able to wreak havoc on the men and their mounts. What had seemed an age of warfare was over very soon. There was not a man nor a tame elephant this side of the clearing. The jungle had been swept clear of humanity. Patches of earth where the sun shone appeared trodden into pulp by the feet of Sirdar's indomitable warriors. Seeing that the destruction wrought by his followers had left wide gaps in the forest growth which helped to expose all of them to the eyes of any hunter who might appear, and ere the tame ones could be rallied again into any kind of an attack, Sirdar sounded the order to retreat.

Like arrows to the heart of a single mark they came rushing to obey him.

Now leaning on Kumar and young Bahadur, the Chief slowly led his herd away from the jungle of Mahapal, where half a dozen of his friends had died in battle.

Though it hurt him to walk he would not desist from carrying out bis entire plan of retreat. They marched all that day and half the night before he would permit anyone including himself to stop. Though every step that he took caused him real agony yet he moved on. Thus he led the herd into the dense forest of Belassore where man had never been seen, nor heard.

That night he had to lie down on the ground in order to sleep, a thing that he had not done ever since his childhood. All these years he had been on his feet, sleeping or waking.

Alas, he was too weak now, so this night of nights he could not remain on his feet. In fact it hurt him excruciatingly even to attempt it, so he resigned himself to sleep on the ground guarded by his son and his followers.

It was about the seventh day after the fateful fight before the Chief could stand up again. Assisted by Bahadur and Kumar he went to a river near by to have his first drink. He then ate chunks of Sahine mud that

Kumar loosened by kicking up the river bank. All three of them ate a quantity of salt. That was done to prevent an attack of dropsy quite prevalent in the climate of Belassore.

In about a fortnight the Chief was well enough to march a few miles a day, a fact which brought gladness to the heart of every member of the herd. So they resumed their journey to their winter quarters further to the south, under the adamantine discipline imposed on them by their leader. All, including Kumar, obeyed him implicitly. For in their heart of hearts they knew that had not his generalship come to their rescue in the nick of time, most of them would be dead by now. Because elephants have the longest memory of all the animals, they can more readily relate an effect to its cause. That is why they never forget their mistakes and missteps. From this point on Sirdar's herd never witnessed any slackening of its sense of discipline.

Here ends the real story of the herd. Sirdar and his friends now belong to those who love an elephant in each and every phase of its growth: first as a child, second as a youth, third as a leader, fourth as a husband and father, and last of all as a selfless person who is ready to give up himself for others. In one word the story of true leadership, whether amongst men or animals, is one of the gradual loss of self. *Selflessness* is the rock on which a leader's life is built. Egoism, vanity, and fear should be as alien to the nature of a leader as life is to death.

publisher's note

Dhan Gopal Mukherji wrote this book, originally published as *Chief of the Herd*, in 1927. He had spent his childhood in Bengal, in a village on the edge of a forest, and perhaps, in this story, he drew on his boyhood observations of forest creatures. The forest features prominently in some of his other books, too, including *Hari the Jungle Lad*, *Kari the Elephant* and *Ghond the Hunter*.

Reading these books, it is clear that Dhan Gopal Mukherji was deeply influenced as a boy by the animals and their ways of living he must have seen around him. His books also present the forests of India as a magical place where the creatures communicate with each other, where animals not just live and die, but where they understand that they are part of a web of life that connects them all.

Some of this has been scientifically proven now. We know that trees can communicate with their kind, and that animals have myriad ways of 'talking' to each other that modern scientists are just beginning to fathom. But some other aspects of the natural world that appear in *Chief of the Herd* are now known to be different from what is written in the book.

Elephant herds are not led by male tuskers, but by a matriarch—a female elephant. Males like Sirdar rarely live in a herd beyond their teenage years. They roam alone, sometimes striking up friendships with other lone males like themselves. But they don't live in a family group and bring up their children, as happens here.

However, it has been known for centuries now that elephants are some of the most intelligent and intriguing of animals. This is why they appear in myths and iegends and folk tales. Elephants hold magic within them—and that magic and majesty is brought to life by Dhan Gopal Mukherji in this book. We hope the reader will be touched by some of that magic through these pages.

Anjana Basu works as an advertising consultant in Kolkata. She writes stories and features in the local newspapers and for *Outlook* and *Statesman*. She is the author of a number of novels, children's books and short story collections. Some of her books for children include *In the Shadow of the Leaves, Leopard in the Laboratory, Eighteen Tides and a Tiger, Hide and Seek Tiger, Lockdown Tiger* and *Chinku and the Wolfboy*. In 2004, she was awarded a Hawthornden Fellowship in Scotland where she worked on her second novel, *Black Tongue*.

Aaryama Somayaji studied Communication Design at the National Institute of Design, Vijayawada. She draws to survive, reads for herself, and eats to stay happy. Illustrating for children is her way of giving back the joy she had as a child. She can usually be found reading in her room or looking at cat videos on the Internet.